Menus à Trois

Menus à Trois

The Soup, Bread, and Salad Cookbook

Julia Older and Steve Sherman

THE STEPHEN GREENE PRESS
LEXINGTON, MASSACHUSETTS

First published in 1987 by The Stephen Greene Press, Inc.
Published simultaneously in Canada by Penguin Books Canada Limited
Distributed by Viking Penguin Inc., 40 West 23rd Street, New York, NY 10010.

The Strawberry Soup recipe on page 24 is used with permission from Lynn Smith.

LIBRARY OF CONGRESS CATALOGING IN PUBLICATION DATA
Older, Julia, 1941–
Menu à trois.
Includes index.
1. Soups. 2. Bread. 3. Salads. I. Sherman, Steve, 1938–   . II. Title.
TX757.042   1987   641.8'13   86-20132
ISBN 0-8289-0599-1

Printed in the United States of America by
R. R. Donnelley & Sons, Harrisonburg, Virginia
Set in Garamond No. 3
Design by Beth Tondreau
Illustrations by Sarah Vure

Contents

Introduction

SOUPS

A friend once told us, "My wife has two hundred cookbooks. She goes through them like I read *Playboy*—neither one of us ever does anything about it."

We hope that the recipes in this book keep you entertained; we also hope that they make you want to do something about them.

Some of these recipes combine ingredients in a natural, likely way. For example, cauliflower and cheese frequently appear together on the American table, so a logical extension is to blend them into a soup. Others started out as international dishes, such as the Indonesian Sateh, and were transformed into soups. All the recipes here evolved in our kitchen and were tested and tasted by us and willing friends.

The Ingredients

Because of the diversity of cultures, the world of food in the United States offers an infinite number of choices for the shopper. Small, isolated backwaters often are within a short drive to cosmopolitan centers that abound in exotic foods ranging from adzuki beans to zampone (Italian sausage stuffed into a boned pig's foot). The recipes in this book, however, don't go out of the way to incorporate extremely rare ingredients. Much of the produce, including celeriac, plantains, radicchio, and kale, can be found in most ordinary supermarkets today. These same markets stock shelves of specialty items, including smoked mussels, caviar, capers, and, in some instances, even truffles. The last few years have been a renaissance in food variety for home cooking.

We live in a town of 1,500 people, but within a short distance we can purchase nopales (the leaf of the cactus eaten in Mexico), fresh chestnuts in season (an Italian specialty), star fruit, mangoes, and papayas (fruits from the tropics), Italian prosciutto, Lebanese sausage, Spanish artichoke hearts, and countless other imported items from Japan, China, the Philippines, France, and elsewhere.

But for those who prefer a reliable basic meal simplicity has not been abandoned in this book. The Pane e Pomodoro Soup is a bread soup, a variation of a recipe that has existed since bread and water. The Creamy Butterbean Soup takes, at most, 15 minutes to prepare and provides a nutritious accompaniment to the fast, spicy, cheesy Busters.

At the same time, we're sympathetic to the mother who ate tabbouleh at a party and bemoaned the fact that her children insisted that "if you can't pronounce it, you can't eat it." If this is the prevalent attitude in your home, you might simply change the name. Fromage de Chevre Soup translated into goat cheese soup may not do the trick, but try offering children green bean soup, which should.

If you're making Pomegranate Soup, draft the children to help you. Chances are that they will be so delighted with the jewel-like seeds that they will look forward to the end result. Some fruits and vegetables, such as jicama, have no American equivalents; however, if you want to introduce it to your children, you might attempt slicing jicama and apple together as an after-school snack. Your children probably won't notice the difference.

Shopping, too, can be an educational experience for the entire family. Youngsters will be intrigued making forages into China-town, little Italy, Greektown, and other ethnic neighborhoods that might be near you. The culture studied in school will come alive through taste. Proust's writings never appealed so much as on the day our French instructor offered each of us a madeleine, which we savored as he read aloud the famous passage about these freshly baked, buttery confections.

During the fourteenth and fifteenth centuries in Turkey, the

Corps of Janissaries guarding the sultan's famed palace, the Seraglio, wore in their caps spoons secured in brass sockets. Their leader, the Chief Janissary, held the title of Head Soup Distributor, and their emblem was a soup kettle. Needless to say, chow was never far from the minds of these soldiers. When the regiments fell on hard times, they would sit outside the gates of the Seraglio and beat on their kettles with spoons. It is easy to imagine them filling their kettles with meals similar to Kishik or Couscous Soup.

Better than banging on a kettle to get your family's attention is to fill it with a sensational soup, such as Shark's Fin Soup or Minted Lamb Lentil Soup, and watch them turn to willing and devoted subjects.

Serving Soups

One of our favorite cooking resource books is Louis P. DeGouy's *The Gold Book*, published in 1947. He advises that "it is often times amusing to see how easily a clever cook can train her household into accepting the most ordinary foods when a little forethought is given to the serving. Dress up your soups."

A can of chicken noodle soup, heated and served with a sprinkle of parsley flakes, will taste like a can of chicken noodle soup whether or not it is disguised with parsley flakes. As we see it, the idea is to serve the freshest ingredients in the most pleasing, aesthetic way. Say that the Red Pepper Soup has been slopped over the rim of the bowl, the bread is sliced so that you can read through it at one end while the other end is an inch thick, and the salad is piled in a jumble on a plate. The difference comes when you now imagine the Red Pepper Soup placed without spills in an attractive white bowl, a uniform piece of Soda Bread with a pat of sweet butter, and a Wild Rice Salad set off in a scalloped green lettuce leaf.

Homemade Broth

There is no real substitute for a full-bodied, flavorful, homemade broth or stock base. Canned broths usually are loaded with salt, yeasts, monosodium glutamate, and a legion of other unnecessary additives. If you're planning a dinner of chicken breast scallops, it is easy to debone the breast and remove the skin with kitchen shears. Add a few cups of water to the skin and bones (simmer it for 20 minutes) and, voilà—chicken broth.

Likewise, leftover roasted chicken, duck, or turkey carcasses and skin may be saved, rinsed, covered with water, brought to a boil, simmered 30 to 60 minutes, salted, strained, poured into plastic containers, and saved for future soups. Turkey makes a wonderful broth; duck tends to be richer and must be degreased.

Fish broths also are easy to make, especially if you buy fish at a market where fishmongers fillet the fish. Fish heads, tails, a bouquet garni, a cup of wine, and a few cups of water all boiled and then simmered 20 minutes or so make a good, quick fish stock. To strengthen it, add a cup of bottled clam juice.

Meat broths may be made with leftover beef bones. In a hurry? We've made half a cup of beef broth from adding water to the pan in which lean ground beef was fried. The best meat broth uses shank and marrow bones, veal, and sometimes fresh stewing beef. Thoroughly brown them to add a dark, rich taste and impart color to the broth.

Recipes for these broths precede the recipes in this book for good reason. They provide the foundation for the soups that follow. Basic broth gives balance and substance to most soups. If you have mastered broths and thought ahead, freezing them for future use, you have done half of your work.

We don't season our broths because recipes usually call for their own seasoning; however, in recipes such as Stracciatelle, Veal Mousse Soup, Miso, Oxtail Consommé Julienne, and other clear broth soups, care should be taken to make the broth as flavorful as possible since it is presented in an unadulterated form.

We urge you to try these simple broths. You'll discover how gimmicky and gummy the store-bought varieties taste in comparison.

Garnishes

Garnishes add a pleasant touch, especially if the soup is a bland color or has a puréed texture. Some soups, such as the Chlodnik, Shark's Fin, and Trout Soup Solianka, include colorful ingredients and textures. The source for the garnishes can be as inventive and extensive as your imagination. Of course, the best garnishes float. Some suggestions for garnishes include the following:

croutons	chiffonade (minced
pasta	greens)
rice	sieved hard egg yolks
barley	toasted cereals
grated cheese	(popcorn)
dumplings	toasted nuts
puffed cereals	bacon bits
sliced lemon	chopped olives
poached eggs	minced fresh herbs
dry toast (Melba style)	small herb ice cubes
whipped cream	marrow balls
sour cream	chicken or
paprika	forcemeat balls

BREADS

Not long ago a connection between what Thoreau said of wood heat and what we were doing—baking bread—dawned on us. In his practical, expansive way, he reminded us that wood warmed him twice, first by cutting it, then by burning it. Bread nourishes us twice, first by making it, second by eating it.

Bread the Aesthetic

The first nourishment comes when deciding what kind of bread to make, gathering the ingredients, mixing the proportions, kneading the dough, shaping the loaf, and baking the bread. You're creating something that didn't exist before, not ripping open a plastic bag packed in a steamy, sometimes seamy, factory. You're making one of the most ancient foods of civilization, an earthy invigoration for all those who eat it, a symbol of friendship and generosity ("companion" derives from "to break bread with"). You are offering a thing you made, not a thing you bought.

This is nourishment of the spirit, the enlivening of yourself as you prepare a loaf of friendly bread, making it with your own hands and effort, doing the best you can, leaving your mark on your handmade gift. (The best gift, says Emerson, is a portion of thyself.)

Making bread well means making bread beautiful. A simple, home-baked loaf of whole wheat can have endearing beauty in its familiar round, dark, crusted shape. So, too, a lush elegance can shine from an egg-glazed Antipasto Braid.

Whatever type of bread you bake, let it come to the table with a sense of aesthetics, framed in a basket, swaddled in a cloth, or spaced handsomely on a platter. Let it come with the irresistible, nutty, bread-baking oven aroma of high-rising wheat slowly toasting to temptation.

The Second Nourishment

The other nourishment is of the body. Baking your own bread gives you more control of what you and others eat. You're the one who chooses what goes into the loaf. You decide whether it's going to be sweet butter or chemical margarine, low-salt or high-salt, lots of sugar or little. You're the one who times the baking for a thin crust or a thick and chewy one.

When you make your own bread, chances are that you won't be putting in chlorine, sodium aluminum sulfate, acetone peroxides, dried eggs, ground dehulled soybeans, polysorbate 60, and other factory agents. Nor will you gas the bread with a chemical that fakes the smell of freshness when you open the plastic bag, as some companies do. The chances are good, too, that you won't mix tree pulp into your wheat, as one national company was discovered doing, calling the bread "high in fiber" without specifying what kind of fiber—sawdust.

The positive reasons for baking your own bread for the good of your body and soul are many, including the true freshness of an oven-direct loaf, the known cleanliness of your kitchen tools, and your chosen quality of ingredients. You do not get these guarantees with bought bread. The plain fact is: the bread we eat is better if it's the bread we bake.

Making It

Baking bread is easy. Some recipes in this book go from mixing bowl to dining table in less than a half hour; others take longer.

Most loaves require two to three hours for the yeast to work. This is an important point, often forgotten: the yeast does the long-term work, and you get the credit. You spend perhaps 15 to 20 minutes mixing and kneading, 5 minutes more shaping the loaves, and the rest of the time on something else, such as making a matching soup and salad.

The unbleached all-purpose flour that we use in many of the recipes is white flour that hasn't been treated with benzoyl peroxide or chlorine dioxide (the leading bleaching agent) to make it un-naturally white. Using stone-ground whole wheat left slightly coarse gives the bread a nuttier taste. Use dry yeast from vacuum-sealed foil packages and small jars, so that the yeast is as fresh as possible. The oil is your preference, but we generally use neutral-tasting safflower oil for the basic loaves (and coating the bowl for the dough rising), corn oil and olive oil for some of the ethnic breads. Sweet butter is fresher and tastier than salted butter and gives more control of the salt content in the recipes, especially for the more delicate breads.

A good way to test a loaf to see if it's baked enough is to remove it from the pan and tap the bottom. If the loaf sounds hollow, it's done. If not, return it to the pan and oven to bake a few minutes more.

A few of the more complicated recipes, such as those for croissants or puff pastry, presume some minimal experience with handling dough, but a challenge is part of the reward.

For the most part, these recipes are simple. The directions are intended to be easy to read, clear, and successful. All they require is that you get your hands into the ingredients and go at it.

SALADS

The salads are designed to take a minimal amount of time and effort for a maximum amount of interesting and appropriate tastes. They are intended to accompany the soups (the main attraction) and the breads (the main accompaniment); so, generally, they are kept simple and direct. In large portions, a few, such as the Salad Niçoise and the Pasta and Smoked Mussel Salad, can be meals in themselves; but overall, the salad recipes are integral to the meal.

More than Lettuce

A lettuce–only salad with prime ingredients and dressing is a classic, but its novelty is limited; therefore, we offer here a variety that ranges from radicchio to jicama salads, wild rice to caviar, white asparagus to tabbouleh. They all play their parts in lending appropriate support for the soups as well as being appetizing in themselves.

With such an array of possible ingredients in this country, a salad becomes more than just a bowl of dressed lettuce. A salad is thought of primarily as a cold dish, but what about the Hot Potato Salad or the Wilted Spinach Salad? Salads are often considered rather mundane necessities, but is this true of Fennel Salad and Belgian Endive Salad? Hardly.

Ingredients for salads are open ended—vegetables (such as Kohlrabi Salad), fish (Crab Salad), meat (Pasta and Sausage Salad), fowl (Chicken and Pea Salad), fruit (Tropical Fruit Salad), grain (Tabbouleh), or some combination (Waldorf Salad, Russian Salad, or Gorgonzola and Apple Salad).

Some are utterly simple and utterly delectable, such as Tomato Wedges with Green Goddess Dressing or White Asparagus Remoulade. Often the simpler *is* the better.

Dressing

We all have our favorite dressing—usually a vinaigrette. Slight variations in the ingredients can make noticeable improvements in taste. Virgin olive oil, walnut oil, or tarragon vinegar can indeed elevate a salad.

Balsamic vinegar, for example, is an aged wine vinegar that provides a mellow tartness rather than merely tartness. The puréed anchovy in the Green Goddess Dressing gives the salad a more subtle undertaste. Fresh lemon juice makes a world of difference over a frozen packaged product; a sugarless, quality mayonnaise (or one you make yourself) builds a more pronounced taste foundation; scallions give a senior taste over the rambunctious yellow onions.

Preparing the majority of the dressings requires few kitchen tools; a few call for a blender or food processor, a grater, a juicer—all simple to use and available. We do find that a tiny whisk helps in blending the basic vinaigrette.

BEVERAGES

The beverages listed following the salads are suggestions only. On one hand, a good dark pilsner beer does go better with the Kielbasa Cabbage Soup, Onion Board, and Cucumber Salad combination than, say, mineral water. On the other hand, you may not like beer, so choose something else.

The list includes wines, beers, teas, fruit juices, vegetable juices, sparkling wines, mixed drinks, espresso, hard spirits, even a tall glass of cold milk, which goes nicely with the Tomato Yam Soup, Apricot Rum Quick Bread, and Waldorf Salad.

You can drink champagne (our favorite) with just about anything at any time. Sweeter wines accompany cream soups better than dry wines. Also, if you serve salads with vinaigrette, we've found that it's better to drink the wine with the soup and bread, not with the salad. Otherwise, a conflict of tastes arises.

USING THIS BOOK

This is a book of suggested complementary soups, breads, salads, and beverages for all seasons. The recipes include hot and cold, spicy and mild, light and filling, fancy and plain, sweet and savory alternatives arranged as complete meals. Feel free to create your own combinations and to rearrange at whim and will.

You may have time for only one soup or one bread or a salad. That, too, is what this book is for—to share with you some of the individual dishes we enjoy making and baking.

—J.O. (Soups and Salads)
—S.S. (Breads and Salads)

Basic Recipes

CHICKEN STOCK

1 lb chicken legs (thigh plus leg)
5 C cold water
1 small carrot
1 small celery stalk
1 sprig parsley
salt to taste

1. Place the chicken, water, and vegetables in a large soup kettle, and bring to a boil.
2. Reduce the heat. Boil slowly for 45 minutes.
3. Salt to taste.
4. Strain the stock. Cool. Skim off all the fat.
5. Strain again through a double layer of wet cheesecloth.

If a clearer stock is required, skim constantly while the stock is cooking.

Yields approximately 4 cups

BEEF STOCK

1 *lb stewing beef*
½ *lb beef marrow bones*
1 *small carrot*
1 *small celery stalk*
1 *small onion, halved*
1 *bay leaf*
2 *sprigs parsley*
3 *black peppercorns*
5 *C cold water*
   salt to taste

1. Brown half the meat in just enough oil to lightly coat the bottom of a heavy skillet.
2. Remove the browned meat, and place it in a soup kettle with all the other ingredients except the salt and water.
3. Pour 5 cups of cold water into the skillet, and scrape the bottom with a spoon to remove all the browned meat juices. Pour this into the soup kettle.
4. Bring to a boil. Reduce the heat and partially cover. Boil slowly 1½ hours or until the meat is tender.
5. Salt to taste.
6. Strain. Cool the stock. Skim off any fat, and pour the stock through a double layer of wet cheesecloth.

Searing the meat until it is dark brown will make the stock a darker color; however, browning the meat seals in some of the juices. This is the reason only half of the meat is browned. Pour in ¼ cup of dry red wine at the beginning of cooking time, if you have it on hand.

Yields approximately 3½ cups

FISH STOCK (FUMET)

1 *lb fish heads (gills removed), tails, bones, skin*
1 *small celery stalk*

2 sprigs parsley
½ C dry vermouth
3 peppercorns
  salt to taste
1 small onion, diced (or 3 shallots)
2½ C water

1. Combine all the ingredients except the salt in a large saucepan. Bring to a boil.
2. Reduce the heat and slowly boil uncovered 15 to 20 minutes.
3. Salt to taste.
4. Strain through a double layer of wet cheesecloth.

Fish stock is strong, so use it sparingly. Try a little in any seafood soup or casserole.

Yields approximately 2 cups

PASTA

½ C unbleached all-purpose flour
½ C semolina
1 egg
1 T olive oil
1 T cold water
  dash of salt

1. Place flour and semolina in a mound on a pastry board. Form a well.
2. Break the egg into the well, and add the oil and water. Add a dash or two of salt.
3. With floured fingers, mix the ingredients together. (Add extra flour if the dough is too sticky to handle.)
4. Knead the dough until it is elastic and smooth. Divide it into three parts.
5. Work each part through a pasta machine roller, or roll it out with a rolling pin until it is as thin as possible (less than ⅟₁₆ inch).

6. Cut the pasta into desired width, and dry on baking sheets for 30 to 60 minutes.
7. Drop into boiling water, and boil until al dente (firm to the bite, not soft). This takes approximately 5 to 7 minutes.

You can either cook the pasta in the soup broth or cook it separately and add it to the soup last.

Yields approximately 2 cups

BASIC BREAD LOAF

2 T yeast
½ C warm water
1½ C water
   pinch of sugar
1 T (scant) salt
2 T oil
5 to 6 C unbleached all-purpose flour (for whole wheat loaves, substitute 1½ C of whole wheat)
   sweet butter

1. Dissolve the yeast in the warm water.
2. Add 1½ cups water, the sugar, salt, and oil.
3. Stir in 3 cups of flour.
4. Mix in 2 more cups flour.
5. Place dough on a flat surface; knead 8 to 10 minutes, adding all-purpose flour to prevent sticking.
6. Place dough in an oiled bowl, turn over so its top is coated with oil, cover with a cloth, and let rise in a warm spot until doubled in bulk (1½ hours).
7. Punch down dough. (Second rising is optional.) On a flat surface, form the dough into a cylinder; and cut into equal halves. Form the loaf by tucking the dough into the bottom center of itself until the top is smooth. Place dough in oiled bread pans, cover with a cloth, and let rise until doubled in bulk (45 to 60 minutes).
8. Bake at 400°F for 25 to 30 minutes or until done. Remove from

the pans, place on a wire rack to cool, and brush the tops with sweet butter.

This water-based bread is foolproof. Its ingredients and method reflect the fundamentals of a wide range of yeasted loaves. A second optional rising before forming the loaves stretches the gluten more for a loftier bread. You can speed up the first rising (not when the loaves are formed) by heating the oven to 150°F, immediately turning the heat off, and placing the dough inside with the oven door shut.

Yields 2 loaves

BASIC VINAIGRETTE

  3 T olive oil
  1 T wine vinegar
     salt and pepper to taste

1. Blend the oil and vinegar.
2. Add the salt and pepper and beat again to dissolve the salt.

BASIC MAYONNAISE

  1 extra large egg
  ¼ t dry mustard
  1 C olive oil
  ½ t salt
     freshly ground white pepper to taste
  1 t wine vinegar or lemon juice

1. Place the egg and mustard in a blender container. Cover and blend one second.
2. Remove the cover and very slowly add the oil drop by drop while blending at a low speed.
3. While the blender is still at a low speed, add the salt, pepper, and vinegar (or lemon juice). If the mayonnaise curdles, you have added the oil too fast. Always refrigerate mayonnaise.

Menus à Trois

Cioppino
Panini
Fennel Salad

The Soup. Cioppino (pronounced chop-eeno) is Italian for a spicy fish stew. The fish and shellfish should be ultrafresh, glistening, and without a "fishy" odor. You may use a lower-priced fish that has a meaty texture to it, such as cusk, monkfish, or bluefish. You can replace the shrimp with scallops, mussels, or even lobster.

The Bread. Panini ("little breads" in Italian) are spongy, crusty, versatile rolls. Serve them fresh and warm with soft sweet butter. Slitting the dough diagonally makes the roll rise in the center; the egg wash gives them a bright shine. Panini freeze well and thaw fast. You can slice them, sweet-butter them, fry them in an iron skillet, and then slather them with red raspberry jam for breakfast. You can also stuff them with nearly any kind of handy sandwich ingredients. Try what we call "links," mustard-coated panini sliced halfway at the side and stuffed with choice sausages.

The Salad. Use Florentine fennel, or finocchio, as you would celery, either braised or chopped raw and eaten. What is especially appealing about finocchio is its mild aniselike flavor that sparks up any lettuce salad. Eaten alone, as in this unadorned rendition, it is utterly refreshing and very simple to prepare.

Drink suggestion: Chianti Classico

Cioppino

½ C virgin olive oil
1½ C peeled and minced onion
3 large cloves garlic, peeled, crushed, and minced
½ C cored, seeded, and diced green pepper
1½ t imported oregano
½ t basil
2 C peeled Italian plum tomatoes (with juice)
2 T hot chile sauce
2 T tomato paste
1½ C Chianti
2 C bottled clam juice
1½ lb meaty fish (blue, monk, wolf, hake)
½ lb shelled and deveined medium-size shrimp
½ t salt
   black pepper, freshly ground

1. Heat the oil in a large enameled or stainless steel soup kettle.
2. Sauté the onions, garlic, green peppers, and herbs in oil over medium heat for 2 to 3 minutes.
3. Cover the kettle, and simmer the vegetables for 10 minutes over low heat, until the ingredients are soft and limp.
4. Add the tomatoes, chile sauce, tomato paste, Chianti, and clam juice.
5. Bring the soup to a boil, and simmer it at a boil for 10 minutes.
6. Cut the fish into pieces, and add it and the shrimp to the soup. Simmer the soup uncovered for 5 minutes.
7. Add salt and freshly ground black pepper. Serve the Cioppino piping hot—but never boil the fish.

Serves 4

Panini

1 T yeast
¼ C warm water
¾ C water
1½ t salt
1 T oil
1 t honey
3 C unbleached all-purpose flour
cornmeal

GLAZE
1 egg white, slightly beaten
1½ T water

1. Dissolve the yeast in the warm water.
2. Add the rest of the water, salt, oil, and honey.
3. Stir in the flour 1 cup at a time.
4. Place dough on a flat surface, and knead for 8 to 10 minutes.
5. Place dough in an oiled bowl, turn over so the top is coated with oil, cover with a cloth, and let rise in a warm spot until doubled in bulk (about 1½ hours).
6. Punch down and shape the dough into a cylinder. Divide into 12 equal parts.
7. Shape each part by forming a smooth ball as you gently stretch and tuck the dough into the bottom center of itself. Now roll the dough between your hands to form a cylinder about 3 inches long. Place on an 18 x 12-inch oiled baking sheet sprinkled with cornmeal. Cover with a cloth, and let rise in a warm place until nearly doubled in bulk (about 45 minutes).
8. With a razor blade or sharp knife, cut a diagonal slit about a quarter of the way deep into the dough from one end to the other across the center of the roll. Beat an egg white with water. Brush panini with the egg glaze.
9. Bake at 400°F for about 15 minutes or until lightly browned. Remove from the oven, and quickly brush on the egg glaze

again. Return panini to the oven for 5 minutes or until you obtain the desired crust texture.

Yields 12 panini

Fennel Salad

1 fennel bulb

DRESSING
6 T olive oil
2 T wine vinegar
  salt and pepper to taste
3 to 4 generous pinches celery seed

1. Slice the white bulb of the fennel horizontally to the stalk into thin rounds. Separate them by hand (they'll break away naturally). Place the pieces in a medium-size, shallow bowl.
2. For the dressing, combine the oil, vinegar, salt, pepper, and celery seed. Pour over the fennel and marinate for 30 minutes. Place the salad on serving plates and chill for 10 minutes before serving.

Serves 4

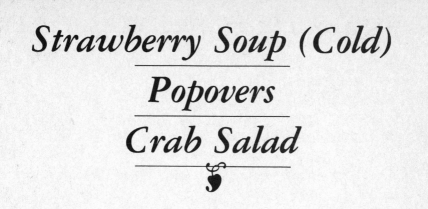

Strawberry Soup (Cold)
Popovers
Crab Salad

The Soup. This recipe comes from the exquisite repertoire of the Café la Fraise restaurant in Hanover, New Hampshire. We were first served this soup in flat, platelike soup bowls with the rim setting off the vibrant roseate color. The ingredients of Strawberry Soup, Café la Fraise, meld together and become one with almost Zenlike concentration.

The Bread. The secret of popover success is to have sizzling-hot tins when the batter first hits them. Also, be sure to have the ingredients at room temperature. We've found that ⅔-cup individual muffin tins measuring 3 inches in diameter and 2 inches deep make four high-and-wide popovers. These crusty-on-the-outside, custardy-on-the-inside, elegant, hollow, singular rolls vent an appetizing little geyser of steam when you tear them open.

The Salad. To make this supremely delicious salad, use scallions, not the large yellow onions, which have too heavy a flavor for this recipe. The fresh dill is a main factor in taste, and fresh lemon juice from a *real* lemon squeezed by hand is essential. Use a sugarless mayonnaise, too. And if you want to make this salad perfect, use fresh-daily Maine crab caught off Cape Rosier on island-filled Penobscot Bay; and watch Judy Ginsburg, whose recipe this is, make and serve it overlooking the rocky Atlantic coast on a sunny, salt air day.

Drink suggestion: kir

Strawberry Soup (Cold)

1½ C water
¾ C Bordeaux
½ C sugar
⅛ C lemon juice
⅛ t cinnamon
1 qt strawberries, hulled, washed, and puréed. (Save 2 whole berries.)
½ C heavy or whipping cream
3 T sour cream

1. Combine the first five ingredients in a saucepan, and boil them uncovered over medium heat for 15 minutes, stirring occasionally.
2. Add the strawberry purée, and boil the soup for an additional 10 minutes, stirring frequently. Skim off any foam.
3. Cool, and chill the soup in the refrigerator for 2 to 3 hours or until it is completely chilled.
4. Prior to serving, whip the cream, and combine it with the sour cream.
5. Fold the cream mixture into the chilled Strawberry Soup.
6. Garnish each serving with half a strawberry.

Serves 4

Popovers

1½ T sweet butter
1 C lukewarm milk
1 extra large egg, at room temperature and slightly beaten
⅞ C unbleached all-purpose flour
¼ t salt

1. Melt the butter, and combine it with the milk in a small bowl. Mix in the egg.
2. Mix the flour and salt in a medium-size bowl.
3. Pour the milk mixture into the flour mixture. Blend thoroughly, but don't overbeat.
4. Brush popover or individual large muffin tins with oil, and heat them on a baking sheet. Let the oil reach the smoking point.
5. Remove the tins on the sheet from the oven, and quickly fill them slightly more than half full.
6. Bake 20 minutes at 450°F. Reduce the temperature to 350°F, and continue baking 15 to 20 minutes.

Yields 4 popovers

Crab Salad

1½ lb fresh crabmeat
3 large scallions, sliced and finely chopped
1 C thinly sliced pickling cucumbers
¼ C chopped fresh dill
juice of 1 large fresh lemon
¾ C mayonnaise
¼ t salt or to taste

1. Place the crabmeat in a large mixing bowl.
2. Mix in the scallions, cucumbers, dill, and lemon juice.
3. Blend in the mayonnaise.
4. Add the salt.
5. Let rest for 2 hours in the refrigerator to allow the flavors to blend.

Serves 4 to 6

Couscous Soup
Lavash
Hearts of Palm

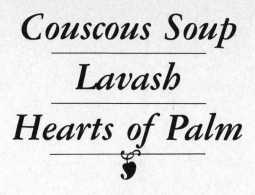

The Soup. This soup cook first tasted couscous in a small Algerian restaurant on the Cours Mirabeau in Aix-en-Provence, France. With the influx of Algerians after the French-Algerian war, couscous became a popular dish. Ideally, you should place the soup in a vessel underneath the couscous so that the grain is steamed over the broth, imparting its flavor. Actually, the word derives from the earthenware pot called a couscousier.

Make sure you buy coarsely ground semolina and not the fine, powdery semolina used by the Italians in their pasta.

The Bread. Called lavash, Armenian flat breads, or cracker bread, these are free-form, thin, crisp, bubbly breads best served plain and warm as accompaniments. Make them any size your baking sheet can hold. Be sure to watch these carefully as they bake because, being so thin, they have little tolerance for cooking and may darken faster than you anticipate.

The Salad. Hearts of palm usually come four to a can. They're smooth, tender, white cylinders from the center of the cabbage palm and are especially popular and prized in South America. If an end seems tough or fibrous from insufficient liquid or processing, simply cut it off. Julienne carrots and celery, plus a few black olives, add an appealing dimension.

Drink suggestion: chilled pear nectar

Couscous Soup

2 T virgin olive oil
1 C peeled and minced onion
½ t ground red pepper
6 C water
1 t salt
1 lb stewing lamb, trimmed and cut into bite-size pieces
2 C peeled tomatoes with juice
3 T tomato paste
2 C peeled and finely diced potatoes
1 C canned chick peas, drained, rinsed, with outer skins slipped off
   under running water
1 C peeled and diced (into ½-inch pieces) fresh eating pumpkin (or
   buttercup squash)
1 C scraped and finely diced carrots

COUSCOUS
2 C couscous (roughly ground semolina)
¼ t salt
¾ C cold water (approximately)
¼ C melted sweet butter
¼ C raisins

1. Place the olive oil in a heavy skillet over medium heat, and
    sauté the onions with the ground red pepper for about 5 minutes.
2. Place all of the remaining soup ingredients (except the couscous)
    in a large soup kettle. Add the sautéed onions. Clean out the
    skillet with some of the soup water, and return it to the soup
    kettle.
3. Cover the soup, and simmer over medium-high heat for 1½
    hours.
4. In a bowl combine the couscous, salt, and some water. Mix it
    well. Gradually add enough cold water to work the couscous
    into a firm ball.
5. Place this ball in the top of a steamer over boiling water. A
    strainer or colander may be used with a lid or cover of aluminum

foil. Steam the couscous approximately 1 hour or until the soup is ready.

6. Place the steamed couscous in a bowl, and break apart the ball until the grains are separated and there are no lumps. Mix in the butter and raisins. Place 2 heaping tablespoons of couscous in each soup bowl, and ladle plenty of soup broth over each portion.

7. Let the soup set for 5 minutes before eating it. This allows time for the couscous to absorb the broth.

Serves 6

Lavash

1 T yeast
¼ C warm water
   pinch of sugar
¾ C water
1½ t salt
1 T oil
3 C unbleached all-purpose flour
   sesame seeds

1. Dissolve the yeast in the warm water in a large mixing bowl.
2. Add the sugar, ¾ cup water, salt, and oil.
3. Stir in the flour 1 cup at a time. Place dough on a flat surface, and knead 8 to 10 minutes.
4. Place dough in an oiled bowl, turn over so the top is coated with oil, cover with a cloth, and let rise in a warm spot until doubled in bulk (about 1½ hours).
5. Punch dough down, place on a flat surface, and shape into a long cylinder.
6. Cut into 10 equal sections. With a rolling pin (and adding flour to prevent sticking), roll individual sections *very* thinly into about 9-inch diameters or lengths (shape doesn't matter).
7. Gently peel from the surface, and place flat with no creases or seams on an ungreased baking sheet. Brush lightly with water. Sprinkle generously with sesame seeds.
8. Bake at 425°F for 5 minutes or until bubbles are well toasted and crisp.

Yields 10 lavash

Hearts of Palm

8 *hearts of palm*
Boston lettuce

DRESSING
4 *T olive oil*
2 *t balsamic vinegar*
salt and pepper to taste

1. Slice each palm heart on the diagonal six times, keeping the slices together in the original whole form.

2. Lay one large choice lettuce leaf on a salad plate. Carefully transfer two hearts to each leaf so that the hearts appear whole.
3. To make the dressing, blend the oil, vinegar, salt, and pepper. Pour over the palm hearts and lettuce.

Serves 4

Duck Gumbo
Saffron Bread
Orange Onion Salad

The Soup. Gombo was the word used in the Congo for the seed pod of the okra plant. When okra was introduced to New Orleans, several changes occurred. Herbs sold by the Choctaw Indians at the French Market were added to the thick okra-based soup.

Duck gumbo is a specialty of the Cajun country of Louisiana. The original recipes call for wild duck from the bayou. Commercial ducks work well, although you must remove the excess fatty skin before you boil them, and carefully degrease the broth. The browned flour sizzles, steams, and lends a dark, rich flavor to the thick gumbo. Place Louisiana hot sauce (Tabasco) on the table for the fire-eaters.

The Bread. Saffron threads give this cakelike loaf its mellow yellow pastel color. The threads are the stamens of the autumn crocus and quickly exude their pleasant staining power in hot water. This loaf is elegant in its simplicity and accompanies this soup nicely. Any leftovers make sumptuous toast just right to spread with apricot jam.

The Salad. Seedless oranges are essential to this recipe; otherwise, your knife won't cut cleanly through for perfect circles. Three onion rings to three orange slices are enough for the characteristic flavor combination; but if you lean toward a zestier taste, double the onions.

Drink suggestion: minted iced tea

Duck Gumbo

2 ducks (4½ to 5 lb each), trimmed of excess fatty skin
  water to cover ducks
¼ lb bacon, sliced and diced
4 T bacon fat, rendered from the bacon
3 T flour
½ C thinly sliced scallions (white part only)
½ C diced celery
¼ C cored, seeded, and diced green pepper
1½ C trimmed and sliced (into ½-inch pieces) okra
1 clove garlic, peeled, crushed, and minced
2 C degreased duck broth
4 C chicken broth
1 t chile powder
1 t Tabasco sauce
1 T Worcestershire sauce
  salt to taste
  cooked rice (½ C per serving)
⅛ C destemmed and minced fresh parsley

1. Place each duck in a large kettle. Cover each duck with water, and place over high heat. Boil. Lower the heat to a simmer, and cover the ducks. Cook 1 hour.
2. Remove the ducks, and place them in a shallow roasting pan to cool to room temperature; then refrigerate. Do this the day before so the grease will solidify for removal. Degrease the broth before using it. Pour off 2 cups of the duck broth for the gumbo; freeze remaining broth for other recipes. (Duck broth is very rich and should be used in moderation or diluted with a lighter broth.)
3. Remove the skin and bones from the duck meat, quite a messy job. Shred the duck into bite-size pieces.
4. Fry the bacon in a heavy skillet over medium heat until 4 tablespoons of bacon fat have been rendered. Remove the crisp

bacon with a slotted spoon, and reserve the pieces. Pour off any excess fat.

5. To the 4 tablespoons of bacon fat, add the flour. Whisk the roux constantly, with the burner on medium-low heat, until it turns smooth and chocolate-colored. The pan will steam slightly. Keep whisking. This roux will take about 4 to 5 minutes to brown under constant surveillance.

6. Add the scallions, celery, green pepper, okra, and garlic to the roux. Sauté the vegetables in the roux for 2 to 3 minutes until they are completely coated.

7. Place the 2 cups of duck broth with the chicken broth in a large, heavy soup kettle. Add the sautéed vegetables, cleaning out the skillet with a little broth to get all of the roux into the soup kettle.

8. Season the gumbo with chile powder, Tabasco, and Worcestershire sauce. Adjust the salt. If the broths are salted, the gumbo shouldn't need additional salt.

9. Cover and simmer the gumbo for 40 minutes over medium heat.

10. Add the duck meat and bacon pieces. Simmer the gumbo another 10 minutes.

11. Serve gumbo over rice with a parsley garnish.

Serves 6

Saffron Bread

2 t saffron threads
½ C boiling water
¼ C sweet butter
1 T yeast
¼ C water
1 T honey
2 T heavy cream
1 extra large egg, slightly beaten
1½ t salt
3 C unbleached all-purpose flour
sweet butter

1. Steep the saffron threads in the boiling water for 5 minutes. Add the butter to melt.
2. Dissolve the yeast in ¼ cup water in a large mixing bowl.
3. Add the honey, cream, egg, and salt to the yeast mixture. Beat in 2½ cups flour, place on a flat surface, and knead 8 to 10 minutes, adding the rest of the flour as needed to prevent sticking.
4. Place dough in an oiled bowl, turn over so the top is coated with oil, cover with a cloth, and let rise in a warm spot until doubled in bulk (about 1½ hours).
5. Punch down dough, knead briefly, shape into a loaf, and place in an oiled bread pan. Cover and let rise until nearly doubled in bulk (45 to 60 minutes).
6. Bake at 375°F for 25 minutes or until done. Remove from the pan, brush the top with sweet butter, and cool on a wire rack.

Yields 1 loaf

Orange Onion Salad

2 seedless navel oranges
1 Bermuda onion
  red leaf lettuce

DRESSING
4 T olive oil
1½ t balsamic vinegar
  salt and pepper to taste

1. Peel the oranges, and remove as much remaining pulp from the outside of the oranges as possible. Slice the oranges into thin rounds.
2. Remove the outer skin of the onion, and slice four thin rounds. Separate these circles into individual rings, discarding the center.
3. On the lettuce leaves, alternate three orange slices with three onion rings for each plate.
4. To make the dressing, mix the oil, vinegar, salt, and pepper. Pour sparingly over each salad and serve.

Serves 4

Rose-colored Cauliflower Soup

Cranberry Orange Loaf

Chicken and Pea Salad

The Soup. Looking at this soup is like seeing the world through rose-colored glasses; the color glows. Cauliflower and cheese sauce long have been a familiar combination on the American table. This recipe takes an ordinary vegetable and blends it into an evocative, distinct taste.

The Bread. Perky cranberries have a spritely tartness and jubilant color in this loaf, and oranges make a savvy partner. A slice of this bread is a deep butter-yellow embedded with bright red nuggets all bordered by a shiny, dark brown, soft crust.

The Salad. Be sure to save the broth that cooked the chicken—perfect for soup bases. Like corn, peas must be eaten very soon after they are picked, before their fragile natural sweetness disappears. So, plant a garden, or get to know someone who did.

Drink suggestion: claret

Rose-colored
Cauliflower Soup

2¼ lb cauliflower, cored and broken into florets
(don't cook larger stems)
salt water
1 T virgin olive oil
3 slices bacon, diced
½ C peeled and minced onion
3 C chicken broth
2 T tomato paste
½ C half-and-half
¼ t paprika
1 C grated and tightly packed cheddar cheese
salt to taste

1. Cook the cauliflower in boiling salt water for 15 minutes or until it's fairly tender. Drain cauliflower and reserve it.
2. In a heavy skillet heat the olive oil, and sauté the diced bacon in the oil over medium heat until the bacon pieces are crisp. Remove them with a slotted spoon, and reserve them for a garnish.
3. Add the onions to the bacon drippings. Sauté the onions over low heat for 2 to 3 minutes. Cover the skillet, and let the onions sweat until they're soft (approximately 5 to 8 minutes).
4. Remove the onions with a slotted spoon, and reserve them.
5. Place 1 cup of the chicken broth, the tomato paste, and all of the drained cauliflower in a blender or food processor, and purée it until smooth.
6. Place the purée in a soup kettle. Add the remaining chicken broth, half-and-half, and paprika to the kettle. Heat the soup over medium heat, but do not boil it.
7. While whisking, slowly add the grated cheese to the soup.

Whisk until the cheese is thoroughly melted. Taste the soup to see if it requires additional salt.

8. Sprinkle each serving with crisp bacon bits.

Serves 6

Cranberry Orange Loaf

1 C fresh cranberries, chopped coarsely
¼ C sweet butter, room temperature
1 C sugar
2 extra large eggs, slightly beaten
1 T orange zest
½ C fresh orange juice
½ C buttermilk
2¼ C unbleached all-purpose flour
½ t salt
1 t baking soda

GLAZE
2 T orange juice
¼ C sugar
1 T sweet butter

1. Prepare the cranberries, and set aside.
2. Cream the butter and sugar.
3. Beat in the eggs. Add the orange zest and juice. Stir in the buttermilk.
4. In a separate bowl, mix the flour, salt, and baking soda.
5. Blend the flour mixture into the butter mixture. Stir in the cranberries.
6. Pour into an oiled 8½ x 4½ x 2½-inch baking dish. Smooth the top. Bake at 350°F for 50 to 60 minutes or until a knife

stuck into the center of the loaf emerges cleanly. Remove from the dish to cool on a wire rack.

7. For the glaze, mix the orange juice, sugar, and butter in a small saucepan. Stirring regularly, boil for 3 to 4 minutes. Brush glaze onto the top of the warm loaf.

Yields 1 loaf

Chicken and Pea Salad

1 C white rice
salted water
½ C fresh peas
1 C shredded cooked chicken
¼ C slivered almonds

DRESSING
6 T olive oil
1 T tarragon vinegar
1 t crushed dried sage
salt and pepper to taste
romaine lettuce

1. Boil the rice in salted water according to directions. Cool thoroughly.
2. Cook the peas 3 to 4 minutes. Cool.
3. In a mixing bowl, combine the rice, peas, chicken, and almonds. Chill.
4. For the dressing, mix the oil, vinegar, sage, salt, and pepper. Pour over the chilled salad. Stir to coat the ingredients.
5. Mound the salad on individual lettuce beds and serve.

Serves 4

Paprikesh Beef Soup
Black Bread
Russian Salad

The Soup. This is a firecracker soup not to be served to delicate constitutions. Hungarian paprika from the czardas country will set you dancing. Because of the saltiness of the ham and sauerkraut and the fiery punch of the paprika, taste the soup before adding salt and pepper.

The Bread. This is an espresso-colored, coarse-grained loaf—you know you're eating hearty country bread. It's a good way to recycle stale white bread. An easy way to toast the crumbs is in an iron skillet over a burner. This is also a good, hefty bread for a baked or grilled Reuben sandwich—corned beef, Swiss cheese, sauerkraut, and Russian dressing.

The Salad. Smoking herring is one of the ancient, traditional methods of curing this cold Atlantic fish. Besides being kippered (smoked and canned in oil), herring now is available in a number of marinades, including sour cream and wine sauce. It's a standard for breakfast on both sides of the Atlantic and should be remembered for salads, too.

Drink suggestion: dark beer

Paprikesh Beef Soup

½ lb stewing beef
4 T corn oil
3 medium-size onions, peeled and diced
3 C beef broth
2 C water
½ t cumin
1 C sauerkraut, undrained
½ C sour cream
2 C plain yogurt
1 T hot imported Hungarian paprika
⅓ lb sliced baked ham

1. Cut the stewing beef into small, bite-size pieces.
2. Heat the oil in a large, heavy soup kettle. Sauté the stewing beef until it is browned.
3. Add the onions. Cover and simmer the meat over low heat for 15 minutes. Stir the meat occasionally.
4. Add the beef broth, water, cumin, and sauerkraut to the soup kettle.
5. Simmer the soup, covered, for 20 minutes.
6. In a bowl mix the sour cream, yogurt, and paprika into a smooth paste.
7. Add this mixture to the soup.
8. Reheat the soup, but don't boil it.
9. Cut the ham into thin julienne strips, and add them to the soup.
10. Serve the soup hot in pottery or crockery soup bowls.

Serves 6

Black Bread

1 T instant coffee
½ C hot water
2 T yeast
1 C lukewarm water
2 t salt
1 T cocoa
2 T oil
2 T blackstrap molasses
2 C toasted bread crumbs
½ C rye
1 C stone-ground whole wheat
1½ C unbleached all-purpose flour
1 t instant coffee
1 T water
cornmeal

1. In a large mixing bowl, dissolve the coffee in the hot water. When the water is warm, dissolve the yeast in the coffee mixture.
2. Add the lukewarm water, salt, cocoa, oil, and molasses.
3. Stir in the crumbs, then the rye, whole wheat, and 1½ cup all-purpose flour.
4. Transfer the dough to a flat surface, and knead for 10 minutes.
5. Shape into a high, rounded loaf and place on an oiled baking sheet sprinkled with cornmeal. With a sharp knife, cut three evenly spaced parallel lines ½-inch deep over the top; then cut two more intersecting lines, forming a grid.
6. Cover with a cloth, and let rise in a warm place until nearly doubled in bulk (about 1 hour).
7. Bake at 400°F for 35 minutes or until done. Five minutes before done, brush the loaf with 1 teaspoon coffee dissolved in water, and return to the oven.

Yields 1 loaf

Russian Salad

tender lettuce greens
2 medium-size potatoes, boiled and thinly sliced
1 Spanish onion, sliced
marinated herring
sour cream

1. Arrange the lettuce greens decoratively in one layer on a serving plate.
2. Place the potato slices in a circle on the lettuce.
3. Place the onion slices on top of the potatoes.
4. Spoon on the herring and some of the marinade in the center of the lettuce.
5. Top the herring with a spoonful of sour cream.

Serves 4

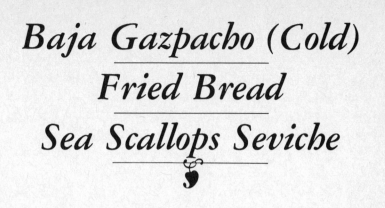

Baja Gazpacho (Cold)
Fried Bread
Sea Scallops Seviche

The Soup. Gazpacho has become a summer favorite from coast to coast, and avocado gives this recipe a distinct Californian identity along with the Spanish/Mexican tastes. If there's not enough time to chill the soup, add an ice cube to each serving.

The Bread. These fanciful breads puff up into unpredictable bubbly shapes. Use tongs to turn them over in the skillet while they're frying. Serve them warm; placing them in a bread basket with a cloth folded over keeps them warm longer. Slathering these breads with butter and honey is a traditional way to eat them. They're also good with confectioners' sugar or cinnamon-sugar sprinkled on right after frying.

The Salad. Cape Cod fishermen tell us that to have the choicest fish dish of all, haul up a scallop, cut open the shell, dangle your feet over the edge of the boat, take a deep breath of the blue-ocean breeze, and pop a fresh one straight into your mouth. Heaven! This salad is at least *close* to the pearly gates. The lime juice "cooks" the scallops, the dressing gives them a confetti look and taste, and the avocado "boats" make you think of Cape Cod—or Baja California—fishermen.

Drink suggestion: sangria

Baja Gazpacho (Cold)

3 C light consommé (1½ C water may be added to double-
  strength consommé to dilute it)
½ C peeled, seeded, and finely diced cucumber
½ C peeled, cored, and finely diced fresh tomato
½ C peeled, seeded, and finely diced avocado
⅓ C cooked, peeled, and deveined small shrimp
⅛ C red wine vinegar
1 T virgin olive oil
1 T peeled and grated (with juice) onion
½ t Worcestershire sauce

1. Place the consommé in a bowl or casserole that has a cover.
2. Add all of the ingredients to the consommé, and chill it, covered,
   for at least 2 hours. Stir before serving.

Serves 4

Fried Bread

1½ C unbleached all-purpose flour
1½ t baking powder
¼ t salt
¼ C dried milk
¾ C warm water
  corn oil

1. Mix the flour, baking powder, salt, and milk.
2. Add the water, and beat the mixture into a dough.
3. Place the dough on a flat surface, and knead a few minutes until

smooth. Cover with a cloth, and let rest for 15 to 20 minutes.

4. Form the dough into a cylinder. Break off egg-size pieces, and roll them less than ⅛ inch thick. Lift the rolled pieces, and stretch them gently into irregular shapes, making a few tissue-thin sections.

5. In 1 inch or more deep hot oil (365°F) in a large skillet, fry on both sides until golden (less than 30 seconds).

6. Remove from the skillet, and transfer to an absorbent paper towel. Serve immediately.

Yields 6 breads

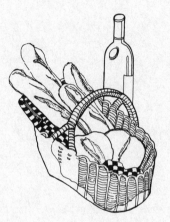

Sea Scallops Seviche

1 dozen sea scallops
  juice of 3 fresh limes

DRESSING
1 T minced onion
1 T finely chopped parsley
3 T diced red pepper
3 T olive oil
  salt and pepper to taste

2 ripe avocados
  red leaf lettuce

1. Cut the scallops into bite-size pieces. Place them in a narrow, shallow bowl, and cover with the lime juice. Let them marinate for 2 to 3 hours. Drain the scallops, reserving some of the lime juice.
2. For the dressing, mix the onion, parsley, red pepper, oil, salt, pepper, and 1 teaspoon of the reserved lime juice.
3. To serve, cut the avocados in half lengthwise, remove the seed, and scoop out the flesh, leaving some of the pulp to act as support for the shells. Reserve the shells. Chop the avocado into the same size as the scallops.
4. Combine the avocado and scallops with the dressing. Spoon the salad into the avocado shells. Place on a bed of lettuce and serve.

Serves 4

Beer Soup
Cheddar Beer Bread
Hot Potato Salad

The Soup. Beer soup is a common refresher course for the colder European countries. Germans and Poles substitute sugar for salt and sour cream or milk for heavy cream. The term *lager* has become a catchphrase for any light-colored beer sold in the United States. A real lager involves a process of aging and the settling of yeasts in the vats.

The Bread. Because the cheese is in a spiral and not saturating the dough, its flavor is more focused instead of overwhelming the entire loaf. The beer is almost undetectable, giving the dough a pliant texture that you'll feel in kneading. Use a fresh Hungarian paprika for some zest in this brunch-type bread.

The Salad. Holding the hot potatoes with tongs or a fork while peeling keeps your fingers cool. As for the bacon, cut it with kitchen scissors before frying or leave the strips whole or in half. This is just as easy and actually gives you better control. The pickle juice adds a more rounded, gentler flavor than straight vinegar. You can prepare the ingredients of this salad far in advance, with the final assembly taking a few minutes in the skillet before serving.

Drink suggestion: German May wine

Beer Soup

2 T sweet butter
⅓ C peeled and minced onion
1 clove garlic, peeled and minced
5 C chicken broth
1 C lager beer
1 C fine white bread crumbs
salt
white pepper, freshly ground
1/16 t freshly grated nutmeg
¼ C heavy cream
1 T destemmed and minced parsley

1. Melt the butter in a heavy skillet over low heat.
2. Add the onions with the garlic, and let them sweat, covered, until they're limp (approximately 5 to 8 minutes).
3. In a medium-size soup kettle, combine the chicken broth with the cup of lager beer.
4. Add the bread crumbs and cooked onions and garlic to the broth.
5. Taste the soup to see if salt is needed.
6. Add the freshly ground white pepper for a zingy taste, along with the nutmeg.
7. Cover the soup, and simmer it for 30 minutes.
8. Add cream just before serving. Reheat but don't boil the soup.
9. Garnish each bowl with a sprinkle of parsley.

Serves 5 to 6

Cheddar Beer Bread

        2   T yeast
      ½   C warm water
    1½   C beer (room temperature)
        1   T (scant) salt
        2   T oil
        2   T honey
        5   C unbleached all-purpose flour
            paprika
        2   C shredded cheddar cheese
            sweet butter

1. Dissolve the yeast in the water.
2. Stir in the beer, salt, oil, and honey.
3. Mix in 3 to 4 cups flour. Place on a flat surface, and knead for 8 to 10 minutes, adding flour to prevent sticking.
4. Place dough in an oiled bowl, turn over so the top is coated with oil, cover with a cloth, and let rise in a warm spot until doubled in bulk (about 1½ hours).
5. Punch down dough, knead 1 minute, and cut into two equal parts. Roll out each part into a ¼-inch-thick rectangle as wide as the size of a bread pan.
6. Sprinkle with paprika to taste. Evenly sprinkle on cheese. Roll up tightly, pinch the seam closed and in a straight line, and place the seam side down in the oiled pan.
7. Bake at 400°F for 25 minutes or until done. Place on a wire rack, and brush the top with sweet butter.

Yields 2 loaves

Hot Potato Salad

2 medium-size potatoes
water to cover

DRESSING
4 rashers lean bacon
½ C chopped onion
⅓ C chopped fresh parsley
½ C dill pickle juice
1 t sugar

1. Cook the potatoes in their jackets in boiling water until done but firm.
2. Remove from the water, and peel the potatoes while they're still warm. Cut into bite-size cubes. Set aside.
3. For the dressing, fry the bacon, and remove to an absorbent paper towel. After it's cooled and crisp, crumble the bacon. Reserve 3 tablespoons of bacon fat in the skillet.
4. Sauté the onions and most of the parsley (reserve 1 tablespoon for the garnish) in the bacon fat.
5. Add the pickle juice and sugar to the onion mixture, and stir. Add the bacon and potatoes; heat thoroughly, stirring with a wooden spoon. Place on warm plates, sprinkle on the reserved parsley, and serve.

Serves 4

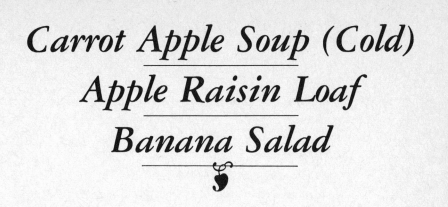

Carrot Apple Soup (Cold)
Apple Raisin Loaf
Banana Salad

The Soup. This is a refreshing, thick, creamy, fruit and vegetable soup with flavors so well matched that at first they are difficult to identify. In order to avoid the slightly granular texture of the apples, first blend the soup and then pass it through the food mill.

The Bread. The extra baking time ensures that the dough surrounding the moist apples is cooked. Consider yourself fortunate if you can find Northern Spy apples; they are tart and good for both cooking and eating. If you have a sweet tooth, brush on a topping of white icing for added splendor. Toast leftover slices under a broiler, and slather with sweet butter for a special Sunday breakfast.

The Salad. Bananas are ripe when brown spots appear on the skins, never before. This is a lightning-fast salad to make and is best when prepared immediately before serving so that the bananas don't discolor, although you can retard this by sprinkling them with lemon or lime juice. Any preferred fruit juice works to thin the mayonnaise and add an undertaste and color.

Drink suggestion: chilled French sparkling white grape juice

Carrot Apple Soup

3 T sweet butter
2 C well-washed and thinly sliced leeks (white part only)
1/8 t marjoram
1/8 t thyme
5 C chicken broth
3 C scraped, washed, and diced carrots
2 C peeled, cored, and diced Granny Smith apples
    salt to taste
1/2 C half-and-half
    nutmeg, freshly grated

1. Melt the butter in a large kettle over low heat, and sauté the leeks in the butter with marjoram and thyme.
2. Cover the leeks, and sweat them for 5 minutes or until soft.
3. Add the chicken broth, carrots, apples, and salt, if needed.
4. Bring the soup to a boil over high heat. Lower the heat, cover the kettle, and simmer the soup for 35 minutes.
5. Cool the soup to room temperature, and refrigerate it overnight.
6. Skim the chicken fat and butter from the top of the soup, and reserve it for other uses. Blend the soup in a food processor or blender for 2 minutes.
7. Transfer the soup to a food mill. Using the finest disk, pass the soup through the mill into a bowl, adding the half-and-half. Chill completely before serving.
8. Grate fresh nutmeg onto each portion.

Serves 4

Apple Raisin Loaf

   2 T yeast
  ½ C warm water
1¼ C water
  2 T oil
  1 T honey
  1 T salt
  5 C unbleached all-purpose flour
  ¼ C sweet butter, melted
  2 t cinnamon
  ¼ C brown sugar
  ⅔ C raisins
  3 cooking apples, peeled, cored, and thinly sliced
    sweet butter

1. Dissolve the yeast in the warm water.
2. Stir in 1¼ cups water, oil, honey, and salt.
3. Mix in 3 cups flour, and beat until smooth. Add the rest of the flour, and knead 8 to 10 minutes.
4. Place dough in an oiled bowl, turn over to coat with oil, cover with a cloth, and let rise in a warm spot until doubled in bulk (about 1½ hours).
5. Punch down dough, and place on a flat surface. Knead 1 minute. Divide into two equal parts. Roll each part into ¼-inch-thick rectangles and as wide as a bread pan.
6. Brush melted butter onto the dough. Mix the cinnamon and sugar; sprinkle onto the dough. Scatter on the raisins. Place the apples one layer thick over the cinnamon-sugar and raisins. Roll up tightly, and place in a lightly oiled bread pan. Let rise 30 to 45 minutes in a warm place.
7. Bake at 375°F for 40 minutes or until done. Remove to a wire rack to cool, and brush the tops with sweet butter.

Yields 2 loaves

Banana Salad

2 peeled ripe bananas
  romaine lettuce leaves
¼ C shelled, roasted, and chopped salted peanuts

DRESSING
⅓ C mayonnaise
1 T sweet cherry juice

1. Slice each banana into four lengths.
2. Place two lengths on each bed of lettuce.
3. Sprinkle with peanuts.
4. For the dressing, mix the mayonnaise and juice. Pour over the salad and serve.

Serves 4

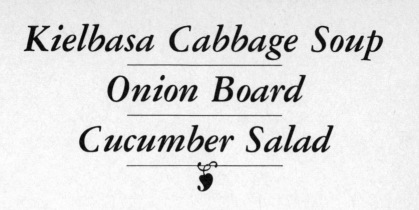

Kielbasa Cabbage Soup
Onion Board
Cucumber Salad

The Soup. Kielbasa is frequently accompanied by cabbage in Poland. The sausage is seasoned with garlic and lends a savory pungency to any soup. Try imported Hungarian paprika, which has a decided edge over other varieties, having been made in that country for more than a hundred years. This soup is a special treat on a cold, blustery day.

The Bread. If you're tantalized by the sweet aroma of butter-sautéed onions and melting cheese, this bread is for you. It's easy to make, addictive to eat. Adding some olive oil to the butter when sautéing the onions helps prevent the fragile butter from burning. You can cut the bread several ways—thick, thin, or diagonally—and remove the crust. Or serve it on a large flat platter or breadboard for a banquet effect.

The Salad. Simple and speedy, this salad, placed artfully on a choice plate, is appealing and refreshing. When shopping, avoid cucumbers with lightish streaks at one end that have turned from white, which is perfectly natural, to yellow, which is a sign of an old cucumber. Look for firm, forest-green cucumbers that slice into crisp rounds. Be generous with the dill (use only fresh dill), because these small threads are what elevate the taste of this salad.

Drink suggestion: pilsner beer

Kielbasa Cabbage Soup

3 C cored and finely shredded cabbage
   salt water to cover
3 C chicken broth
3 C water
1 lb kielbasa Polish sausage
¾ C peeled and diced onion
1 garlic clove, peeled, crushed, and minced
2 C peeled whole tomatoes (with juice)
1 t salt
2 t Hungarian paprika
½ C dry white wine

1. Cover the cabbage with water. Blanch the cabbage for 15 minutes over high heat in boiling salt water.
2. Place all of the other ingredients in a separate soup kettle, and bring them to a boil. Reduce heat to a simmer.
3. Drain the cabbage, and add it to the soup kettle.
4. Cover the kettle, and simmer the soup for 45 minutes at a slow boil.

Serves 6

Onion Board

1 T yeast
1 C warm water
pinch of sugar
1½ t salt
1 T oil
3 C unbleached all-purpose flour
1½ C chopped onion (1 to 2 large white onions)
2 T sweet butter
1 T olive oil
¾ C shredded mild cheddar cheese
⅓ C grated Romano cheese
cornmeal

1. Dissolve the yeast in the water.
2. Add the sugar, salt, and oil.
3. Stir in the flour. Knead on a flat surface for 8 to 10 minutes, adding flour only to prevent sticking. Form the dough into a round, place it in an oiled bowl, turn it over to coat the top with oil, cover with a cloth, and let rise in a warm spot until doubled in bulk (about 1½ hours).
4. Meanwhile, sauté the onions in the butter and oil in an iron skillet over medium-low heat. Cover the onions, and let them steam until transparent (about 10 minutes). Set aside to cool.
5. Punch down the dough, and roll it ½ inch thick into a 14 x 10-inch rectangle. Transfer it to an oiled baking sheet sprinkled with cornmeal.
6. Spread the onions over the dough. Sprinkle on the cheeses.
7. Bake at 400°F for 20 minutes or until done.

Yields 1 loaf

Cucumber Salad

1 medium-size cucumber, peeled, notched, and sliced
  salt to marinate

DRESSING
4 T olive oil
1 T balsamic vinegar
  salt to taste
2 t snipped fresh dill leaves
⅓ C sour cream

1. After peeling and before slicing the cucumber, deeply—and decoratively—gouge the tines of a fork along the length and circumference of the cucumber. Then lay the slices on a large plate or platter, and lightly sprinkle with salt. Set aside for 5 to 10 minutes.
2. For the dressing, blend the oil and vinegar in a small mixing bowl. Mix in a pinch of salt. Mix the dill and sour cream.
3. Add the cucumber slices, and turn them with a wooden spoon to coat them. Arrange 10 to 12 slices attractively on each salad plate, and serve chilled.

Serves 4

Celeriac Soup
French Wreath Bread
Pasta and Sausage Salad

The Soup. France and Belgium have a particular liking for this winter vegetable that looks like a large turnip and tastes like celery. There's a reason. Celeriac (pronounced sel-laír-ee-ak) is a versatile soup and stewing vegetable, blending well with other vegetables and giving off a sweet, subtle flavor of celery. The smaller celeriac knobs are more flavorful and not as tough. You can grow celeriac in your home garden. This soup includes all the ingredients of a vichyssoise, and you'll enjoy it chilled or hot.

The Bread. This festive-looking bread is easy to cut or break off in any size you wish. When you braid the bread, try to keep the weave snug. You can start the braid in the middle of the three ropes, and then turn it over to finish the other ends; but we find this method too troublesome, not to mention that turning it over sometimes tilts the braid out of shape. It's better to simply start at one end and proceed to the other, making sure that each braid is symmetrical to the preceding one. Wreath breads make endearing centerpieces.

The Salad. Rotini are springy, spiral pasta that have lots of surface area for the dressing. This is an easy-on-the-palate salad with hidden subtle scallions, mild sausage flavor, and bright green flecks of parsley.

Drink suggestion: ale

Celeriac Soup

3 T sweet butter
1 C well-washed and thinly sliced leeks (white part only)
$\frac{1}{16}$ t thyme
  dash of white pepper
1$\frac{1}{2}$ lb celeriac (about 4 C peeled and diced)
1 C peeled and diced potatoes
5$\frac{1}{2}$ C turkey or chicken broth
$\frac{1}{2}$ C heavy cream
  fresh parsley, destemmed and finely minced

1. In a large skillet, melt the butter over medium heat, and sauté the leeks a few minutes. Add the thyme and white pepper. Turn the heat to low, cover the skillet, and sweat the leeks 2 to 3 minutes.
2. Peel and dice the celeriac. Add the potatoes and celeriac to the skillet. Stir, cover, and cook them about 10 minutes, stirring occasionally. Don't let the mixture brown.
3. Heat the broth in a large soup kettle. Add the vegetables, and bring the soup to a boil. Reduce the heat to medium. Cover and simmer the broth and vegetables for 20 minutes.
4. With a slotted spoon, place half the vegetables in a blender or food processor and pour in half the liquid. Blend it until smooth, and pour the purée into a bowl. Repeat.
5. Pour all of the blended soup back into the soup kettle. Add the cream and heat the soup thoroughly. Taste and correct for salt. Sprinkle parsley on each portion as a garnish.

Serves 6

French Wreath Bread

2 T yeast
½ C warm water
1½ C water
1 T salt
2 T oil
  pinch of sugar
5 to 6 C unbleached all-purpose flour
  cornmeal

GLAZE
1 egg white
1 T water

1. In a large mixing bowl, dissolve the yeast in the warm water.
2. Add the rest of the water, the salt, oil, and sugar.
3. Beat in 3 cups of flour. Add the rest of the flour, and place on a flat surface. Knead for 8 to 10 minutes, adding flour to prevent sticking.
4. Place dough in an oiled bowl, turn over so the top is coated with oil, cover with a cloth, and let rise in a warm spot until doubled in bulk (about 1½ hours).
5. Punch down dough, and form into a cylinder on a flat surface. Divide in half. Divide each half into three equal sections.
6. To form the wreath, roll each of three pieces between your fingers and thumb, gently stretching and narrowing the dough until the "ropes" are 36 inches long. Place the ropes side by side and braid them, alternating placing each outside rope between the other two. Place the braid in a circle on an oiled baking sheet

sprinkled with cornmeal, and then pinch the ends together to form the wreath.

7. Cover and let rise until doubled in bulk (about 45 to 60 minutes).
8. Brush the top with the egg glaze. Bake at 400°F for 15 minutes. Brush again with the egg wash. Bake another 5 minutes or until done.

Yields 2 loaves

Pasta and Sausage Salad

2 C cooked rotini pasta
2 T finely chopped scallions (4 medium-size)
8 thin slices of Lebanese sausage (about ⅛ lb)
2 T chopped fresh parsley

DRESSING
6 T olive oil
1 T balsamic vinegar
salt and pepper to taste

green leaf lettuce leaves
4 fresh parsley sprigs

1. Place the rotini in a mixing bowl.
2. Chop only the white parts of the scallions, and add them to the rotini.
3. Cut the sausage rounds in half, and then cut them into ½-inch wide strips. Add to the rotini mixture.
4. Add the chopped parsley. Mix the ingredients. Chill.

5. For the dressing, mix the oil and vinegar. Season to taste. Immediately before serving, pour the dressing onto the salad; and stir to coat the ingredients.
6. Spoon the salad onto the lettuce bed. Top with parsley sprigs.

Serves 4

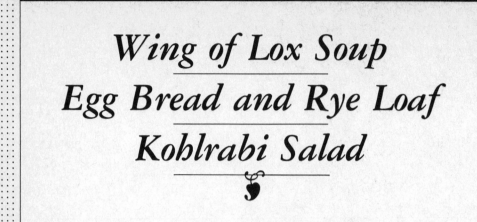

Wing of Lox Soup
Egg Bread and Rye Loaf
Kohlrabi Salad

The Soup. In the States, many food ingredients that people of other countries consider delicious and useful are thrown away. Most fish markets dispense with the fins (wings), tails, and backbones of fresh salmon and smoked lox because nobody asks for them. Sometimes the fishmongers will gladly give these ingredients to you for a song (or possibly even without the song). This soup does have fishbones; however, if you are eating *en famille*, nobody will care if you pick out the bones. Leave a plate on the table for this purpose. Quantities need not be exact, and alter the soup by substituting vegetables to your taste.

The Bread. Cut the loaf for a surprise layer of dark rye across a slice of rich egg bread. Make both breads at the same time. Since the rye takes longer to rise, urge the dough along to be ready for forming with the egg bread by using the oven; turn the heat on until it reaches about 150°F, and then turn it off. Put the rye in the oven to rise. This versatile loaf matches any number of sandwich ingredients, too.

The Salad. Also known as turnip cabbage, kohlrabi has a gentle white turnip flavor. Look for the small size, under 3 inches in diameter; they're the sweetest and don't need peeling. The kohlrabi core grows above ground into an exotic satellite-looking globe with "antennae" stems for support.

Drink suggestion: bock beer

Wing of Lox Soup

2 lb wing of lox
6 C cold water
2 medium-size potatoes, peeled and quartered
2 medium-size carrots, scraped and cut into 1-inch pieces
2 stalks celery, threaded, with leaves, and cut into 1-inch pieces
2 small onions, peeled and cut into quarters
  salt and freshly ground black pepper to taste
  sour cream

1. Rinse off the lox or fresh salmon. You may discard the head if cooking it doesn't appeal to you. Place the salmon in a large soup kettle, and add the cold water. Bring it to a boil over high heat. Lower the heat, cover the kettle, and simmer the broth ½ hour.

2. Prepare the vegetables. Add them to the soup pot. Simmer them at a slow boil for another ½ hour.

3. Taste the soup to see if it needs salt. Smoked lox usually is heavily salted; fresh salmon is not. Start with 1 teaspoon of salt for fresh salmon, and add more if necessary. Add pepper to taste.

4. Make sure that each person is served pieces of salmon and some of each vegetable. Remind diners to watch out for fishbones. Serve with dollops of sour cream for a garnish.

Serves 6

Egg Bread and Rye Loaf

EGG BREAD

1 T yeast
¾ C warm water
  pinch of sugar
1½ t salt
1 T oil
2 extra large eggs
3½ C unbleached all-purpose flour

1. Dissolve the yeast in the water.
2. Add the sugar, salt, oil, and eggs.
3. Stir in 3 cups flour in thirds. Place on a flat surface, and knead 8 to 10 minutes, adding flour to prevent sticking.
4. Place dough in an oiled bowl, turn over so the top is coated with oil, cover with a cloth, and let rise in a warm spot until doubled in bulk (about 1½ hours).
5. Punch down dough, place on a flat surface, and divide into four equal pieces. Roll each piece to fit an oiled bread pan. Place one part in each of two bread pans. Place a rye part on top (see following directions) and then the other two parts each on top of the rye pieces.
6. Let rise until nearly doubled in bulk (about 45 to 60 minutes).
7. Bake at 400°F for 20 to 25 minutes or until done.

RYE

1 T yeast
¾ C warm water
1 t salt
1 T oil
1 T molasses
1 t caraway seeds
1 C medium-ground rye flour
1 C unbleached all-purpose flour
  sweet butter

1. Dissolve the yeast in the water.
2. Add the salt, oil, molasses, and caraway seeds.
3. Beat in the rye flour.
4. Blend in the all-purpose flour. Place on a flat surface, and knead for 8 to 10 minutes, adding flour to prevent sticking. The dough will be puttylike.
5. Place dough in an oiled bowl, turn over so it is coated with oil, cover with a cloth, and let rise in a warm spot until doubled in bulk (about 1½ hours).
6. Punch down dough, and divide into two equal parts. With a rolling pin, roll each part to fit the bread pans. Place each rye section on top of an egg bread part in the two pans.
7. Let rise until nearly doubled in bulk (about 45 to 60 minutes).
8. Bake at 400°F for 20 to 25 minutes or until done. Cool on a wire rack. Brush the tops with sweet butter.

Yields 2 loaves

Kohlrabi Salad

4 kohlrabi (the size of lemons)
water to cover

DRESSING
¼ C olive oil
1 T wine vinegar
2 T tomato juice or tomato-based vegetable juice
½ small clove garlic, peeled and pressed
¼ t salt
black pepper, freshly ground (2 twists of the mill)
green leaf lettuce

1. Cut away the stems from the kohlrabi bulb, and peel away any tough outer skin if the bulbs are more than 3 inches in diameter. Slice the kohlrabi into ¼-inch-thick rounds. Cut the rounds in half.
2. Cook the slices in lightly boiling water until tender (about 10 to 15 minutes).
3. Drain the kohlrabi, and cool.
4. For the dressing, mix the oil, vinegar, tomato juice, garlic, salt, and pepper.
5. Place the kohlrabi slices on a bed of lettuce, and pour on the dressing.

Serves 4

Chestnut Soup
Waffles
Fruit Salad

The Soup. You'll spend some time hulling the chestnuts. Be sure to wear plastic gloves to save your fingernails. If desired, make the purée in advance and freeze it for future use. Putting the creamy nut soup in mugs keeps it hot for a living room fireside appetizer or stand-up buffet; however, offer spoons to your guests, because the soup thickens as it settles.

The Bread. You should remember waffles for their light, crisp, butter-and-syrup-drenched simplicity. Use sifted cake flour, extra large eggs, sweet butter, and room-temperature egg whites. Try to serve waffles immediately; warming them in an oven while you prepare others softens them. Or make a small batch and, just before serving, fit them back into the iron for a moment to crisp them again. You can gild the lily by topping waffles with small, fresh strawberries and wild blueberries or add ingredients to the batter, such as fried bacon pieces, sour cream, or chopped walnuts. In the end, however, authentic maple syrup can't be topped.

The Salad. This salad has all the familiar pleasures; but out-of-the-ordinary fruits, such as mangoes, star fruit, figs, dates, and others, work well, too. For eye appeal, cut the fruit in about the same size but into different shapes for each fruit.

Drink suggestion: sauterne

Chestnut Soup

1½ lb chestnuts
1 T corn oil
hot water
½ t salt
5 C chicken broth
dash of white pepper
dash of paprika
½ C heavy cream
⅛ t dry mustard
salt to taste
3 T sherry
½ C heavy cream
½ t sugar
sprinkle of ground walnuts

BOUQUET GARNI
3 sprigs celery
4 sprigs fresh parsley
1 small piece bay leaf
⅛ t dried thyme (or one sprig fresh)
1 clove
cheesecloth
kitchen thread

1. Using a sharp paring knife, score the rounded part of each chestnut with a crisscross. Wear gloves and be careful; the shell is tough.
2. Preheat the oven to 450°F.
3. Place the oil in a large, 10-inch iron skillet or any other shallow, ovenproof receptacle with a handle.
4. Place the chestnuts in the skillet, and put it in the oven.
5. Shake the chestnuts occasionally, remembering to use a potholder. In 10 to 15 minutes the chestnuts will burst open and sizzle. Take them out and cool them just long enough so that

you can handle them. Remember to wear a potholder when you remove them from the oven as well. Peel them with a knife, removing the outer and inner skins.

6. Make the bouquet garni.
7. Place the chestnuts in a medium-size saucepan. Cover them with hot water, and add ½ teaspoon of salt and the bouquet garni.
8. Bring the chestnuts to a boil. Lower the heat to medium, cover the pan, and simmer them at a slow boil for 25 minutes. The chestnuts should be soft.
9. Discard the bouquet garni, and drain the chestnuts.
10. Using the finest disk of a food mill, grind the chestnuts into a bowl. This will take muscle, unless you use a cup or so of the chicken broth to ease the chestnuts through.
11. There should be about 3 to 4 cups of chestnut purée.
12. Place the remaining chicken broth in a soup kettle. Add the purée to the broth along with a dash of white pepper and paprika.
13. Heat the soup over medium-low heat until it has boiled once. Remove from heat and stir in ½ cup cream and the dry mustard. Add salt to taste and the sherry. Whip the cream with the sugar. Serve soup in mugs with a dollop of whipped cream sprinkled with nuts.

Serves 6

Waffles

1¾ C sifted cake flour
½ t (scant) salt
2 t baking powder
3 extra large eggs, separated
¼ C sweet butter
1½ C milk, room temperature

1. In a medium-size bowl, mix the flour, salt, and baking powder.
2. Beat the egg whites until stiff.
3. Beat the egg yolks until creamy and lemon colored.
4. Blend melted and cooled butter and the milk into the beaten yolks.
5. Pour the yolk mixture into the flour mixture, and stir to a marbled texture; don't overblend to a paste.
6. With a rubber spatula or wooden spoon, fold the egg whites into the batter. Transfer to a spouted glass measuring cup.
7. Pour onto a hot, seasoned, ungreased waffle iron, and cook until steam stops escaping (about 6 to 8 minutes). Gently lift the iron to see if the waffles are cooked to your taste—golden or nutty.

Yields 8 waffles

Fruit Salad

1 navel orange, peeled, sectioned, and cubed
1 Bartlett pear, sliced and cubed
1 banana, peeled and sliced
1 sweet apple, quartered, cored, sliced, coarsely chopped

¼ C halved purple seedless grapes
1 kiwi, peeled and sliced
   lemon juice

DRESSING
1 cucumber, peeled and seeded
1 t fresh lemon juice
2 T mayonnaise
2 T heavy cream
   salt and white pepper to taste

1. Prepare the fruit, place it in a large mixing bowl, sprinkle with lemon juice, and chill.
2. For the dressing, chop the cucumber, place in a saucepan, cover with water, and boil for 5 to 7 minutes.
3. Drain, place in a blender, and purée.
4. To the cucumber purée, add the lemon juice, mayonnaise, cream, salt, and pepper.
5. Pour the dressing onto the fruit, and stir gently with a wooden spoon to coat the ingredients. Serve in fruit cups.

Serves 6

Hominy Buttermilk Soup
Sage Bread
Corn and Red Pepper Salad

The Soup. This recipe combines many ingredients used by native Americans. Hominy is dried corn that has been hulled after soaking in lye. Pine nuts also are in extensive use, and five million pounds are gathered annually from piñon trees by southwestern Navajos and Pueblos. The cowboys out on the range used dried beef, or charqui (a Peruvian word); and it became known as jerky. Today, the beef is pickled like corned beef, dried, and processed with salts and nitrates, then machine sliced.

The Bread. This moist, soft bread has a wonderful sage pungency. Be patient. It rises slowly. Between your fingers crush the sage leaves into as fine particles as you can. This aromatic bread is delicious many ways—toasted, spread with jelly, used for chicken or turkey sandwiches, or just plain buttered.

The Salad. This salad is utterly simple and utterly toothsome, colorful, and all-American. Prepared this way, the peppers are relatively soft—partially cooked and with the tough skin removed. It's best to use truly fresh corn but difficult to muster it fast enough from field to table. If you can manage, pick your own corn and rush it to your kitchen, because the natural sugar turns to starch in about a half hour.

Drink suggestion: cranberry juice

Hominy Buttermilk Soup

1 T corn oil
¼ lb salt pork, diced into ½-inch pieces
½ C peeled and minced yellow onion
½ C pine nuts
2 C chicken broth
5 oz dried beef
  warm water
½ t cumin
2 C drained and rinsed canned white or yellow hominy
2 C buttermilk

1. In a large, heavy soup kettle, heat the oil. Add the salt pork, and render the fat over medium heat. The pork dice will turn brown. Remove the pieces with a slotted spoon, and discard them.
2. Add onions to the fat, and stir 1 minute. Reduce the heat. Cover the kettle, and let the onions sweat for 5 to 8 minutes.
3. Place the pine nuts with the chicken broth in a blender or food processor, and thoroughly blend them to a creamy consistency.
4. Slice the dried beef into ½-inch strips, and soak it in a bowl of warm water.
5. After the onions are tender, squeeze the water from the dried beef, and add it with the cumin to the onions. Stir and sauté the beef over medium heat until it is frizzled and curled.
6. Add the pine nut mixture to the beef, and bring it to a boil. Reduce the heat, and simmer for 5 minutes.
7. Add the hominy and buttermilk. Heat well, but do not boil.

Serves 4

Sage Bread

1 T yeast
¼ C warm water
1 extra large egg, slightly beaten
1 C cottage cheese
1 T vegetable shortening
2½ C unbleached all-purpose flour
1½ t salt
   pinch of sugar
¼ t baking soda
2 t crushed dried sage

1. In a small bowl, dissolve the yeast in the water.
2. In a medium-size bowl, beat the egg, cheese, and melted shortening together until well blended. Add the yeast mixture.
3. In a bread bowl, combine the flour, salt, sugar, baking soda, and sage.
4. Pour the egg mixture into the flour mixture. Stir until a stiff but thoroughly blended dough is formed. Briefly knead the dough together in the bowl. Brush the top of the dough with oil, cover with a cloth, and let rise in a warm place until nearly doubled in bulk (about 1½ to 2 hours).
5. Place dough on a flat surface, and knead briefly. Place in an oiled, round, 1-quart glass baking dish; cover; and let rise 1 hour.
6. Bake at 350°F for 30 minutes or until done.

Yields 1 loaf

Corn and Red Pepper Salad

2 *sweet red peppers*
1 *large ear of sweet corn*

DRESSING
corn oil
salt

1. To prepare the peppers, place them on a baking sheet about 3 to 4 inches from the broiler, and let them get scorched black in as many places as possible. Watch them as they broil (the part closest to the broiler will burn the outer skin first; the inner part won't burn). Turn them with tongs. This process takes about 10 to 15 minutes. Remove the peppers from the oven, and immediately wrap them in a thick cloth towel. The contained heat will steam the burned skin loose. When the peppers are cool, slip the skins off with your fingers. Remove the stem and seeds, then cut the softened peppers into julienne strips.
2. To prepare the corn, remove the husk and, with a sharp knife cutting vertically, remove the kernels. Place the kernels in a steamer or a covered strainer over boiling water, and steam for 5 minutes. Cool.
3. To serve the salad, place the pepper strips in parallel lines on a plate. Artfully sprinkle on the corn kernels.
4. For the dressing, lightly drizzle oil over the salad. Sprinkle lightly with salt. Serve.

Serves 4

Pomegranate Soup
Feta Crescents
Lentil Salad

The Soup. The skin of the pomegranate should be glowing red and shiny. The fruit is usually available from September through December. First cultivated in Persia, pomegranates have crimson, glowing, jewel seeds sheathed by the leathery skin, always a delightful surprise. Extricating the seeds from the intricate honeycomb web isn't an easy task. Perhaps a fascinated child might join in the pleasure of seeking the treasured rubies. The taste of this soup conjures visions of walled gardens and splashing fountains, and serenades the palate with pleasing exotic tastes.

The Bread. Feta is a goat cheese packed in brine, which makes it salty. To reduce the salt, soak the cheese in milk for 15 minutes before using. After baking, simply break off from the roll any feta that may have melted and cooked onto the baking sheet. A mainstay of Greek kitchens, feta gives these crescents a pronounced, exuberant taste.

The Salad. An ancient Mediterranean food, lentils are a versatile, nutritious legume (they're high in iron and protein) and are much quicker to prepare than their cousins, the beans and peas. Lentils usually are used for soups and stews, but they're equally pleasing when cooked and chilled for salads.

Drink suggestion: chilled apricot juice

Pomegranate Soup

1 lb chicken quarters (leg and thigh)
5 C water
¼ C threaded and diced celery
4 scallions, thinly sliced (white part only)
1 t salt
3 pomegranates
1 lb eggplant, peeled and cubed
2 T sugar
2 T fresh lime juice

1. Place the chicken in a soup kettle. Add the water, celery, scallions, and salt. Bring the chicken to a boil, reduce the heat, and cover the kettle. Simmer it for 20 minutes.
2. Meanwhile, cut the pomegranates in half, and carefully push the seeds from the integument and outer skin. Reserve the seeds in a bowl.
3. Using the medium-size disk of a food mill, process the seeds. This will provide about 1 cup of pomegranate juice.
4. Prepare the eggplant.
5. Remove the chicken from the soup kettle. Let it cool, then pick the meat from the bones. Discard the skin and bones. One pound of chicken quarters will yield approximately 2 cups of chicken meat.
6. Add the pomegranate juice, chicken meat, and eggplant to the soup kettle. Reheat the soup to boiling, cover the kettle, and simmer it over medium heat for 20 minutes.
7. Stir in the sugar and fresh lime juice; serve the soup piping hot.

Serves 4

Feta Crescents

1 T yeast
½ C warm water
  pinch of sugar
1 t salt
¼ C sour cream
2 T chopped fresh chives
2 C unbleached all-purpose flour
¼ lb feta cheese, crumbled

1. Dissolve the yeast in the water.
2. Stir in the sugar, salt, sour cream, and chives.
3. Mix in the flour. Knead 8 to 10 minutes, adding minimal amounts of flour to prevent sticking.
4. Place dough in an oiled bowl, turn over so the top is coated with oil, cover with a cloth, and let rise in a warm spot until doubled in bulk (about 1½ hours).
5. Punch down dough, and shape into a flat oval. With a rolling pin, roll into a very thin circle, 10 inches in diameter.
6. Cut wedges with 3-inch-wide ends on the circumference of the circle.
7. Sprinkle feta on the wedges. Starting with the wide end, loosely roll up the crescent so that the end point rests on the bottom of the crescent.
8. Place the crescents on an oiled baking sheet. Cover with a cloth, and let rise until nearly doubled in bulk (about 45 minutes).
9. Bake at 400°F for 10 to 15 minutes or until lightly toasted and done.

Yields 6 to 8 crescents

Lentil Salad

½ C lentils
  salted water
1 T chopped scallions (1 medium-size scallion)
3 T chopped parsley (reserve 4 sprigs for garnish)
2 T sliced and diced carrots
  green leaf lettuce

DRESSING
4 T olive oil
1½ t balsamic vinegar
¼ t dry mustard
  salt and pepper to taste

1. Cook the lentils covered with 2 inches of salted water until tender (about 30 minutes).
2. Drain the lentils, and cool.
3. Mix the scallions, parsley, and carrots into the lentils.
4. For the dressing, blend the oil, vinegar, mustard, salt, and pepper. Pour over the salad, and spoon onto the lettuce bed. Chill before serving.

Serves 4

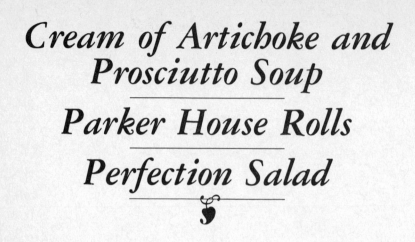

Cream of Artichoke and Prosciutto Soup

Parker House Rolls

Perfection Salad

The Soup. This soup falls into the "Hurried Gourmet" category. Artichoke hearts come packed in oil or in brine (water and salt). The Spanish artichokes often are very tender. Taste some of the leafy part of the artichoke heart to make sure the vegetable isn't tough or stringy. If it is, trim the hearts down to the soft, delectable part. Most large delicatessens carry Italian-style dried prosciutto ham. Unfortunately, the real thing doesn't exist in this country because of health regulations.

The Bread. These classic dinner rolls originated from the venerable 1855 Parker House Hotel in downtown Boston. Served in the stately, high-ceilinged, wood-paneled dining room, they became the absolute prototype—light, soft, not too sweet, perfectly folded over about two-thirds, and a treat to eat. They take a little practice to make a batch in uniform size and shape, but that's the fun.

The Salad. This old-time salad from the "gelatin fifties" has lost fashion, but its confetti-like coloring, glistening shape, and vibrant taste leap over any current vogue. You can make it far ahead of a meal, and it will still look bright and fresh.

Drink suggestion: fresh orange juice mixed with sparkling white wine

Cream of Artichoke and Prosciutto Soup

2 T clarified sweet butter
½ lb prosciutto (Italian ham), thinly sliced, trimmed of fat, and cut into ½-inch strips
2 T flour
2 C milk
1 C heavy cream
16 oz artichoke hearts preserved in brine, drained, and cut into small pieces
dash of white pepper
¼ t salt
nutmeg, freshly grated
½ C grated Parmesan cheese

1. Butter is clarified by heating it until the solids separate, leaving the translucent fat on top, then removing the milky solids. Heat the clarified butter in a large saucepan. Add the prosciutto, and sauté it over medium-low heat for 1 to 2 minutes.
2. Add the flour, and stir it with a wooden spoon so that the ham is evenly coated. Slowly add 1 cup of the milk, stirring constantly. Heat the ham 2 to 3 minutes, then add the remaining milk.
3. Heat the soup to just below boiling, making sure to stir. Add the heavy cream, artichokes, pepper, salt, and a dash of nutmeg. Do not boil this soup, but make sure it's piping hot.
4. Before serving, sprinkle Parmesan on each portion.

Serves 4

Parker House Rolls

1 C milk
1 t salt
1 T sugar
1 T sweet butter
1 T yeast
¼ C warm water
1 extra large egg, slightly beaten
3½ C unbleached all-purpose flour
¼ C sweet butter, melted

1. In a small saucepan, combine the milk, salt, sugar, and 1 tablespoon butter. Heat and stir until the last three ingredients are dissolved. Cool to lukewarm.
2. In a large mixing bowl, dissolve the yeast in the warm water.
3. Pour the cooled milk mixture into the yeast mixture. Stir in the egg. Add 2½ cups flour, and beat 100 strokes. Add the rest of the flour, place on a flat surface, and knead for 5 minutes, adding flour to prevent sticking.
4. Place dough in an oiled bowl, turn over so the top is coated with oil, cover with a cloth, and let rise in a warm spot until doubled in bulk (about 1 hour).

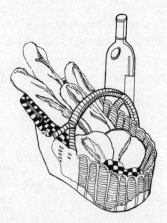

5. Punch down dough, and place on a flat surface. Roll the dough to a ½-inch thickness. Using a 2-inch biscuit cutter or glass, cut out the rolls. Brush the top with the melted butter. With a sharp knife, slightly cut the roll (not all the way through) and a bit off center. With the knife across the dough, pull the shorter half of the roll over the knife, stretching the dough and turning the knife flat as you pull. Pinch the edges together.
6. Place the rolls nearly touching each other on an oiled baking sheet. Let rise 15 to 20 minutes.
7. Bake at 375°F for 18 minutes or until lightly browned and done.
8. Remove them to a wire rack to cool. Brush the tops with the rest of the melted butter.

Yields 18 rolls

Perfection Salad

½ C chopped celery
½ C shredded carrots
½ C shredded cabbage, soaked in vinegar water
   for 15 minutes and drained
½ C chopped sweet green pepper
2 T chopped pimiento
1 T gelatin
1¼ C water, divided
¼ C sugar
½ t salt
¼ C vinegar
   romaine lettuce

1. Prepare the vegetables, and set aside.
2. Soften the gelatin in ½ cup of cold water in a saucepan. Blend in the sugar, salt, and vinegar.
3. Add ¾ cup boiling water, and stir to dissolve the gelatin. Chill until it's the consistency of unbeaten egg whites (about 45 to 60 minutes).

4. Fold in the vegetables, and pour into four small, individual, custard-type molds. Chill until set. Turn onto a bed of lettuce and serve.

Serves 4 to 6

Veal Mousse Soup

Crumpets

White Asparagus Remoulade

The Soup. This is an unusual, light soup with Italian flavors. You can substitute boned chicken breasts for the veal. Veal Mousse Soup will cheer up a child or adult confined to bed and offers a variation from the standard ho-hum chicken soup. This green-topped mountain in a sea of golden broth satisfies the eye as well as the palate.

The Bread. Crumpets are similar to English muffins, but they have softer, tastier insides. The dough can be sticky to manage, but this is what gives crumpets their special texture. So stick with it! After the crumpets are cool, separate them horizontally into halves with a fork to preserve the "holey" texture. Then toast them, and layer on soft sweet butter.

The Salad. The dressing is a variation of a remoulade (without the anchovy paste) and enlivens this specially grown asparagus. A 15-ounce can or jar contains an ample number of spears.

Drink suggestion: Earl Grey tea

Veal Mousse Soup

½ lb uncooked sliced veal, scallopine-style thin cut
3 eggs
½ C grated Parmesan cheese
⅛ t salt
  black pepper, freshly ground
1 T virgin olive oil
1 small clove garlic, peeled, crushed, and minced
½ lb well-washed and destemmed fresh spinach
4 C chicken broth (or half chicken and half veal broth)

1. Place the veal in a food processor (or a blender) with the eggs, adding them one at a time. Purée them into a paste. This will take approximately 30 seconds.

2. Add the grated Parmesan to the veal, and blend another 30 seconds. Add the salt and a dash of pepper. Purée another few seconds.

3. Heat the olive oil in a large, heavy kettle over medium heat.

4. Add the garlic to the oil. Sauté it for a few seconds, then add the spinach. Cover the kettle.

5. Cook the spinach over medium-low heat, stirring it occasionally. It should be limp and tender in approximately 5 to 8 minutes.

6. Drain the spinach in a strainer, pressing out the juice with a spoon.

7. Place the spinach on a chopping board, and chop it well with a mezza luna or sharp knife.

8. Butter four custard cups (or ovenproof individual molds). Place 1 tablespoon of spinach in the bottom of each cup.

9. Add the veal mixture, leaving some space at the top of the cup. Place the cups in a Pyrex container with shallow sides. Fill the container with water so that it reaches halfway up the sides of the cups.

10. Place the cups in a preheated 325°F oven for 15 minutes. Test the mousse with a knife. The knife should come out clean; when it does, the mousse is ready.

11. Heat the broth to boiling. Ladle the broth into each bowl. Loosen the mousse from the cups by running a knife along the edge. Invert the cup or mold over the soup bowl so the mousse falls into the broth, spinach side up.

Serves 4

Crumpets

½ C milk
½ C water
1 T yeast
   pinch of sugar
1 t salt
1¾ C unbleached all-purpose flour
¾ t baking soda
1 T room-temperature water

1. In a small saucepan, heat the milk and water together until warm. Transfer to a bread bowl.
2. Sprinkle the yeast to dissolve in the warm milk mixture. Add the sugar.
3. Mix the salt into the flour, and stir into the yeast mixture. The dough will be sticky. Cover with a cloth, and let rise in a warm place until doubled in bulk (about 1½ hours or less).
4. In a measuring cup, dissolve the soda in the water, then stir into the dough. Let rise again until doubled in bulk (about 45 to 60 minutes or less).
5. Place oiled, 4-inch muffin rings on a lightly oiled griddle or cast-iron skillet. Heat to low-medium (slow heat ensures that the centers of the crumpets are cooked without burning the

outsides). With a large kitchen spoon, scoop up the dough, which will be sticky and bubbly, and place it inside the rings about 1 inch deep. Don't try too hard to smooth the dough; it will expand to fill the rings as the crumpets cook.

6. Cook very slowly—about 15 minutes on the first side. When the underside is brown and the top is slightly crusty to the touch, turn over the rings with a spatula. Cook the second side until lightly browned (about 5 minutes).

7. Remove crumpets from the skillet, remove the rings, and cool the crumpets on a wire rack.

Yields 6 crumpets

White Asparagus Remoulade

16 *white asparagus spears*
   Boston lettuce leaves

DRESSING
½ *C mayonnaise*
¾ *t Dijon-style mustard*
 1 *T minced dill pickle*
 1 *t drained and chopped capers*
 2 *t finely chopped parsley*
 1 *t finely chopped fresh chives*
¼ *t finely chopped fresh tarragon*

1. Place the asparagus spears attractively across the lettuce leaves. Chill.

2. For the dressing, mix the mayonnaise, mustard, pickle, capers, parsley, chives, and tarragon; and chill. Before serving, drape the dressing across the asparagus.

Serves 4

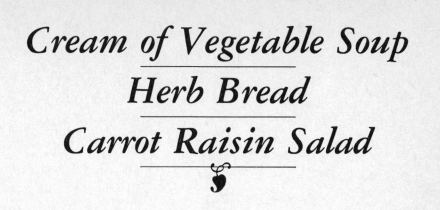

Cream of Vegetable Soup
Herb Bread
Carrot Raisin Salad

The Soup. This soup takes approximately 10 minutes to make if you prepare the veal broth ahead of time. Freeze any remaining veal broth for use in other recipes. Cream of Vegetable Soup can be a warm comforter during winter blizzards or a chilled refresher during the dog days of summer.

The Bread. This pungent bread forms a dark, thick, chewy crust and is singular for its sturdy taste. It interlocks nicely with this soup and salad. Also, because of its complex flavor, the bread makes wonderful sandwiches. Try it, for example, with sliced cold roast leg of lamb and layers of red leaf lettuce, a spread of quality mayonnaise, and a hint of mint jelly. Or make a Vermont cheddar cheese sandwich fried slowly in sweet butter with crisp homemade dill pickles inserted over the melted cheese.

The Salad. Balsamic vinegar can darken a brightly colored salad, so a different vinegar, such as a cider-based one, works better with many ingenious salads such as this one. Try to chop the walnuts the same size as the raisins for eye and tongue harmony. This salad is best when served with a very light touch of dressing.

Drink suggestion: orange pekoe tea

Cream of Vegetable Soup

2 C cooked diced vegetables (see veal broth, p. 98)
1½ C veal broth
2 T sweet butter
2 T flour
1 C half-and-half
salt to taste
nutmeg, freshly grated

1. Pass the vegetables through the fine disk of a food mill. Add the veal stock to the vegetable purée, and stir it well.
2. Melt the butter in a saucepan over medium-low heat, and whisk in the flour to make a roux.
3. Slowly add the half-and-half while whisking the soup constantly as the béchamel sauce thickens.
4. Add the puréed vegetables and broth to the cream sauce; heat the soup, but don't boil it.
5. Add salt to taste (approximately 1 teaspoon if the broth isn't salted). Sprinkle the soup with nutmeg.

Serves 4

Herb Bread

½ C chopped fresh parsley
2 T chopped fresh chives
2 T yeast
½ C warm water
½ C water
1 T (scant) salt
2 T corn oil
pinch of sugar
1 C unflavored yogurt
1½ C whole wheat
4 C unbleached all-purpose flour
butter
cornmeal

1. Prepare the herbs, and set aside.
2. Dissolve the yeast in warm water in a large mixing bowl.
3. Add ½ cup of water, salt, oil, sugar, and yogurt. Stir in the herbs.
4. Stir in the whole wheat and 2 cups of all-purpose flour. Add the rest of the flour, place on a flat surface, and knead for 8 to 10 minutes.
5. Place dough in an oiled bowl, turn so that the top is coated with oil, cover with a cloth, and let rise in a warm spot until doubled in bulk (about 1½ hours).
6. Punch down dough, place on a flat surface, and shape into a cylinder. Cut into three equal parts. Round out the loaves by turning and tucking the dough into itself at the bottom until smooth on top. Place the loaves on oiled baking sheets sprinkled with cornmeal, and cover with a cloth. Let rise until nearly doubled in bulk (about 45 minutes).
7. Bake at 400°F for 25 minutes or until done. Place on a wire rack to cool. Brush with melted butter.

Yields 3 small loaves

Carrot Raisin Salad

2 C shredded carrots (loosely packed)
½ C chopped walnuts
½ C (scant) raisins

DRESSING
3 T walnut oil
1 t apple cider vinegar
   salt and pepper to taste

1. Mix the carrots, walnuts, and raisins together.
2. In a separate small bowl, blend the oil, vinegar, salt, and pepper.
   Immediately before serving, pour onto the carrot mixture, and
   toss lightly to coat.

Serves 4

Chlodnik (Cold)

Pretzels

The Soup. To say chlodnik (shlud-nick) is almost as satisfying as eating it. Chlodnik (sometimes called cholodziec) is a cold, soured, uncooked borscht made in the old country with fermented beet juice. A delightful cookbook sent to us by a Polish friend states, "The most elegant addition is cooked shelled tails of crayfish. Unsuccessful attempts have been made to substitute shrimp, but Lithuanian chlodnik and shrimps are two different worlds irreconcilable in one pot." So make for your favorite lake to snare those crawdaddies. Although served cold, chlodnik isn't a light summer soup, but a substantial meal combining the salad (garnishes) with the soup (borscht) in a tantalizing mixture of textures and tastes.

The Bread. The intertwined double loop is the most familiar pretzel shape; but plain, straight sticks, rings, or other forms of your whim work as well. Pretzels have a long history dating back to Roman times. They supposedly warded off evil if worn around a person's neck or beckoned good if snapped in ritual like turkey wishbones. This recipe produces crisp, not soft, pretzels. Boiling them in the baking soda solution gives them a special pretzel taste. Coarse sea salt is essential.

Drink suggestion: Czechoslovakian beer

Chlodnik (Cold)

1 lb well-scrubbed beets
water to cover
5 C well-washed, destemmed, and coarsely chopped beet greens
(approximately 5 tightly packed cups)
¼ C destemmed and minced fresh dill
½ C dill pickle juice
1 t sugar
1½ C veal broth (see following)

VEAL BROTH
2 lb veal shanks
12 C cold water
1 C peeled and diced onions
1 C scraped and diced carrots
1 C threaded and diced celery
8 black peppercorns, crushed and tied in cheesecloth

GARNISHES
1 C cooked veal (from above), cut into bite-size pieces off the
shank bones
2 hard-boiled eggs, peeled and sliced
½ lb peeled and deveined cooked crayfish tails (shrimp may be
substituted)
1 C sour cream
1 C peeled, seeded, and diced cucumber

1. Leave 1 inch of the stem on the beets so that they don't bleed
   as much. Boil them in water to cover until they are tender
   (approximately 20 minutes).
2. Reserve 2 cups of the cooking water from the beets.
3. Place the beets under cold running water, and slip off the skins
   and stems with your fingers.
4. Place the cooked beets and greens in a large kettle. Cover
   them, and cook down the greens over low heat (approximately

5 to 8 minutes). Stir them occasionally so they don't burn and stick. Add a little of the cooking water from the beets if necessary.

5. In a blender or food processor, purée the beets, greens, and dill with 2 cups of cooking water from the beets.

6. Add the dill pickle juice and sugar to the beet mixture, and stir it well.

7. To make the veal broth, place the veal shanks in 12 cups of water with the onions, carrots, celery, and peppercorns. Bring them to a boil, and remove any foam with a slotted spoon. Simmer the broth, covered, for 1 hour.

8. Remove the veal shanks to a separate bowl to cool.

9. Strain off 1½ cups of the veal broth, and reserve the remaining broth and vegetables for Cream of Vegetable Soup (see p. 94) or other recipes.

10. Add the 1½ cups of veal broth to the beet chlodnik, and refrigerate it for 3 to 4 hours or until it is well chilled.

11. Place the garnishes in serving bowls, or arrange them on a serving platter set in the center of the table. White bowls best offset the brilliant beet color.

Serves 4

Pretzels

1 T yeast
1 C warm water
  pinch of sugar
1 t salt
3 C unbleached all-purpose flour
1 T baking soda
2 qt water
1 extra large egg, beaten
  coarse salt
  sesame seeds

1. Dissolve the yeast in the water.
2. Add the sugar and salt. Mix in the flour. Knead 8 to 10 minutes until smooth and elastic. Place dough in an oiled bowl, turn over so the top is coated with oil, cover with a cloth, and let rise in a warm spot until doubled in bulk (about 1½ hours).
3. Punch down dough, and form into a cylinder. Cut off walnut-size pieces, and roll and stretch them with your hands; do this either on a flat surface or between your thumb and forefinger. Stretch the dough to 18 inches and pencil-thin.
4. To form into the traditional pretzel shape, lay the dough in a shallow arc, bringing the ends toward you. Twist the ends around each other completely to form a double hook in the center of the pretzel. Gently pinch the ends equidistant to the central part of the arc. You should have three empty spaces in the pretzel. Place the pretzels on an oiled baking sheet.
5. Add the baking soda to 2 quarts of boiling water. Carefully drop the pretzels into the water by hand or with a flat skimmer, spatula, or slotted spoon. Remove them with the skimmer after they rise to the surface and enlarge slightly (about 30 to 60 seconds). Return the pretzels to the baking sheet.
6. Brush the egg onto the pretzels. Add salt sparingly to all sections of the pretzels by pressing on the crystals with your finger. Do the same with the sesame seeds.
7. Bake at 425°F for 12 to 15 minutes or until well browned. Cool on a wire rack.

Yields 2 dozen pretzels

Miso
Shrimp Crackers
Daikon Salad

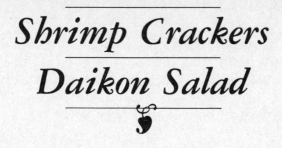

The Soup. Miso is a paste made from fermented soybeans and sea salt. The Japanese use it to enhance flavor and also as a thickener. (Many health food stores carry a "light miso" with less salt.)

Miso should remain a light, clear soup with just enough vegetables so that you can still see the bottom of the bowl. Start with this version and then try adding other vegetables, such as slices of sautéed fresh mushrooms, celery, or broccoli spears. Tofu also is made from soybeans. Make sure that it is well sealed and dated for freshness.

The Bread. These are simple, crisp wafers that are quick to make. You can more likely find the shrimp paste at Japanese and Chinese stores. The paste is ground shrimp blended with oil, salt, and pepper. You can find the rice flour at most natural food stores.

The Salad. Daikon is a large, snow-white, watery, spindle-type (as opposed to round) radish. Also known as Chinese radish, its slight peppery aftertaste sends a pleasant tang through your mouth. Keep everything simple with this salad, from presentation to serving plate to dressing.

Drink suggestion: green tea

Miso

4 scallions
1 C well-washed and destemmed fresh spinach leaves
2 T vegetable oil
4 C chicken broth or beef broth (or half-and-half)
1 T miso soybean paste
½ lb tofu, cut into small ½-inch squares

1. Trim the scallions, leaving 3 inches of green leaves. Cut the scallions into small ¼-inch rounds.
2. Pack the spinach tightly to measure 1 cup; then slice or shred.
3. Heat the oil over medium heat in a soup kettle. Sauté the scallions for 2 minutes; then add the spinach, and stir it until it wilts.
4. Add the chicken broth to the vegetables. If you have freshly made the broth, don't salt it. Heat the soup.
5. Pour off ½ cup of the hot broth, and mix in the miso paste.
6. Add the miso mixture to the soup. Heat it to just boiling.
7. Divide the tofu into each bowl.

Serves 4

Shrimp Crackers

1 C rice flour
½ t salt
¼ t baking soda
1 extra large egg white
2 T shrimp paste
2 T milk
coarse salt

1. Mix the rice flour, salt, and baking soda.
2. Beat the egg white until foamy. Stir in the shrimp paste to disperse it. Add the milk.
3. Pour the egg mixture into the rice mixture, and beat it into a stiff dough. Use your hands to form a ball of the dough. Knead briefly on a flat surface.
4. Roll out the dough very thinly (the dough will be stiff). With a 2-inch round cutter, cut out the crackers. Place them on an oiled baking sheet. Prick the tops of the crackers with a fork. Brush the top with water, and sprinkle with coarse salt.
5. Bake at 375°F for 5 to 7 minutes or until done.

Yields 16 crackers

Daikon Salad

2 C slivered daikon
   slivered carrot

DRESSING
2 T safflower oil
2 t white rice vinegar
   salt to taste

1. Prepare the daikon by peeling away the outside skin. Slice into 3-inch strips ¼ inch thick. With a vegetable peeler, gently sliver the daikon into very thin, nearly translucent strips.
2. Prepare the carrot by peeling away the outside skin. Slice into similar-size strips as the daikon. Peel very thin slivers from the

outer layer of the carrot (stop short of the central root section). Add very few carrot slivers to the daikon, only enough to highlight the featured radish.

3. For the dressing, blend the oil, vinegar, and salt. Pour over the salad, mix well, and serve.

Serves 4

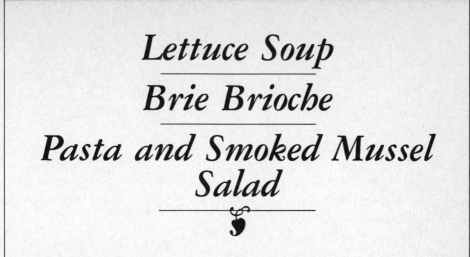

Lettuce Soup

Brie Brioche

Pasta and Smoked Mussel Salad

The Soup. Lettuce isn't just for salads; it makes an elegant, light soup, too. The French dote on creme de laitue soup, and you can find many recipes. By trial and error, you will discover that the lettuce should be of a buttery Boston variety; and you need not cook it long to impart the mild yet absorbing flavor.

The Bread. Many have said that brioches originated in Brie, France, and that these luscious butter-and-egg-rich rolls were made as a matter of course with Brie cheese, which also originated in Brie. (Another theory holds that these rolls were named after their baking methods—"bris" {to break} and "boucher" {to stir}.) Tradition has warped the subtlety of brioche au fromage with strong-tasting shredded Gruyère or cheddar, but you'll find that this version rekindles some of that sublimity with the special shy undertaste of the Brie. The topknot, the jaunty "hat" of good cheer, is the traditional signature of petite brioche.

The Salad. Search for fresh, pencil-thin asparagus, the most tasty size. The snow peas (or sugar peas) should be small, too, for the sweetest taste. You may have often used smoked mussels as hors d'oeuvres; but tossed in such a bright-looking salad as this, they add a smooth, delicious, dark taste.

Drink suggestion: chilled fumé blanc

Lettuce Soup

8 C *finely shredded and tightly packed Boston lettuce*
3 T *sweet butter*
4 T *flour*
2 C *milk*
½ t *salt*
3½ C *chicken broth*
½ t *sugar*
4 T *sweet butter*
½ C *heavy cream*

1. Four firm heads of Boston lettuce will yield approximately 8 cups of shredded chiffonade. Pick off the outer loose leaves; then wash each lettuce head by spreading the leaves and running water on them. Cut the heads of lettuce in half, core them, and roll the leaves tightly while cutting finely into shredded strips.
2. Make a béchamel sauce in a medium-size saucepan. Melt 3 tablespoons of butter, and whisk in the flour over low heat. Add milk and salt, constantly whisking to prevent lumping and sticking. Simmer but don't boil the sauce until it is thick.
3. In a large bowl combine 2 cups of the béchamel, the chicken broth, and sugar.
4. Melt 4 tablespoons of butter in a casserole or soup kettle. Add the lettuce, coat it with butter, cover it, and cook it until it wilts (approximately 3 minutes).
5. Add the béchamel mixture to the lettuce, and simmer it uncovered over medium heat for 10 minutes.

6. Place a food mill over a large bowl; with the fine disk in place, pass the soup through the mill.
7. Return the soup to the soup kettle, add the cream, and heat it well; but do not boil.

Serves 6

Brie Brioche

1 T yeast
¼ C warm water
1 T sugar
1½ t salt
3 large eggs, slightly beaten
2¼ C unbleached all-purpose flour
¼ lb sweet butter, room temperature
⅓ lb 60% double-cream Brie, crust removed, room temperature

GLAZE
1 egg yolk
1 T heavy cream

1. Dissolve the yeast in the water in a large bread bowl.
2. Add the sugar, salt, and eggs.
3. Beat in the flour. To knead, grab the dough and, literally, throw it again and again into the bowl for 10 minutes. The dough will be sticky, but the pulling, grabbing, and throwing gradually stretch and elasticize the dough.
4. Squeeze pieces of all the butter into the dough.
5. Squeeze pieces of the Brie into the dough, dispersing it as smoothly as the butter.
6. With a wooden spoon, scrape down the inside of the bowl.

Smooth and consolidate the dough. Cover with a cloth, and let rise at room temperature until doubled in bulk (1½ to 2 hours).

7. Punch down and chill the dough in the bowl for 30 minutes.

8. Place the dough on a floured flat surface, and cut off a quarter of the dough to reserve for the topknots. Divide the remainder into 8 to 10 pieces (depending on the size of the molds). Round up the pieces and place them in ungreased, fluted, petite brioche or muffin tins.

9. For the topknots, first scissor a deep gash in the center of the dough in the molds. Divide the reserved dough into the 8 or 10 parts, and shape each one into rounds with a small cone tip on the bottom. Fit the point into the gash of the dough in the molds, and press down gently to secure in place. Let rise 30 minutes.

10. For the glaze, mix the egg yolk and cream. Brush onto the brioches.

11. Place the molds on a baking sheet, and bake at 450°F for 15 minutes or until done.

Yields 8 to 10 rolls

Pasta and Smoked Mussel Salad

> 2 *C seashell pasta*
> *salted water*
> 8 *very thin asparagus spears*
> 12 *snow peas*
> 1 *small tomato*
> 3 *oz prepared smoked mussels*

DRESSING
¼ *C olive oil*
2 *t balsamic vinegar*
1 *t dry mustard*
1 *chopped scallion*
  salt and pepper to taste

  red leaf lettuce

1. Cook the pasta in salted water, and drain. Rinse under cold running water, and drain again. Dry and chill.
2. Slice off the stems of the asparagus; remove the stems from the snow peas. Steam the asparagus and snow peas (they may be steamed together only if the asparagus spears are very thin). Slice the asparagus straight across into bite-size pieces. Slice the snow peas on the diagonal.
3. Quarter the tomato, and cut into bite-size cubes.
4. Place the pasta in a large bowl; mix in the asparagus, snow peas, and tomato.
5. Drain the mussels, and pat off some of the oil with an absorbent paper towel. Add to the pasta mixture.
6. For the dressing, mix the oil, vinegar, mustard, scallion, salt, and pepper. Pour over the salad, and stir to coat the ingredients. Serve on beds of lettuce.

Serves 4

Stracciatelle
Antipasto Braid
Gorgonzola and Apple Salad

The Soup. Stracciatelle literally means rags in Italian, and this soup does have a sort of ragged appearance. The Chinese call it egg-drop soup. The broth should be strong and flavorful, and you can season it to your liking. High in protein, low in calories, this soup is light, quick, and easy on the cook.

The Bread. The finished loaf glistens a dark brown from the egg wash, and the braid gives it a classic touch of architecture. You can roll the dough on the baking sheet, but this becomes more cumbersome than transferring it to the sheet later. Cappicola is pepper-flavored prepared pork sliced translucently thin and combines well with provolone and spinach to help make this a special savory loaf—ideal for the soup here. Substitute prosciutto, if you wish, but we find that the fattier, fuller-flavored cappicola heightens the overall taste of the loaf better than the more subtle prosciutto.

The Salad. Leaving the skins on two different kinds of apples adds some color to pique the eye. A burgundy-colored Empire apple and a lime-green Granny Smith, for example, make a smart combination that's tasty as well.

Drink suggestion: espresso

Stracciatelle

2 eggs (room temperature)
1 T lemon juice
2 T grated Parmesan cheese
1 small clove garlic, peeled and crushed
2 C chicken broth
2 C beef broth
salt and pepper to taste

1. Combine eggs, lemon juice, cheese, and garlic in a bowl; and mix minimally with a fork so that the white and yolk of the eggs are still fairly separate.
2. Combine and simmer the broths. Bubbles should not break the surface. You can also boil the broth and then turn off the heat.
3. Hold the egg mixture approximately 5 inches above the broth. Have a fork ready in the other hand. Pour the egg mixture in a slow, steady stream and break it in midair with the fork. This will produce strands of egg in the broth. Taste for salt and pepper.
4. Serve the stracciatelle immediately.

Serves 4

Antipasto Braid

1 T yeast
1 C warm water
pinch of sugar
1½ t salt
1 T oil
3 C unbleached all-purpose flour
10 to 12 oz cooked, drained, and chopped fresh spinach
1 T olive oil
½ t dried dill
salt to taste
½ lb thinly sliced cappicola
¼ lb thinly sliced provolone

GLAZE
1 egg yolk
1 T water
1 t poppy seeds
cornmeal

1. In a bread bowl, dissolve the yeast in the cup of warm water.
2. Add the sugar, salt, and oil. Stir in the flour. Remove dough from the bowl, and knead for 8 to 10 minutes, adding flour to prevent sticking.
3. Place dough in an oiled bowl, turn over so the top is coated with oil, cover with a cloth, and let rise in a warm spot until doubled in bulk (about 1½ hours).
4. Prepare the spinach, and place in a bowl. Stir in the olive oil, dill, and salt. Set aside.
5. Punch down the dough, and place on a flat surface. Roll out the dough to a 14 x 10-inch rectangle; shape the edges evenly with your hands.
6. Spread the spinach down the length of the middle third of the dough. Top the spinach first with the cappicola and then the provolone.

7. With a serrated knife, cut the dough into strands 1-inch wide on both sides of the filling. Now alternately fold each strand over the filling on a slight diagonal; the strands will overlap one another partially, enclosing the filling. Pinch and seal the ends of the loaf, if necessary.
8. Place loaf on an oiled baking sheet sprinkled with cornmeal.
9. For the glaze, mix the yolk and 1 tablespoon of water, and brush the top of the loaf. Sprinkle on the poppy seeds.
10. Bake at 400°F for 25 minutes or until done.

Yields 1 loaf

Gorgonzola and Apple Salad

1 red apple, cored and cubed
1 green apple, cored and cubed
green leaf lettuce

DRESSING
½ C crumbled Gorgonzola cheese
¼ C olive oil
2 T fresh lemon juice
1 scallion, finely chopped
½ T Dijon-style prepared mustard
salt and pepper to taste

1 T chopped parsley

1. Prepare the apples, and place them in a salad bowl with enough torn lettuce for four servings.
2. For the dressing, mix the cheese, oil, lemon juice, scallions, mustard, salt, and pepper. Pour over the salad and mix.
3. Sprinkle on the parsley.

Serves 4

Truffle Soup
Puff Pastry
Tomato Wedges with Green Goddess Dressing

The Soup. Unearthed, the truffle looks somewhat like a shri-veled-up black nut that some squirrel forgot he'd buried. So why all the fuss over this chlorophyll-less fungus? Taste. No one can describe it. So, our advice to you is to live it up and go on a treasure hunt through the markets for a canned Perigord truffle.

Try this soup first before inviting guests. The puff pastry is a bit tricky. You must tie it to the dish with kitchen string; oth-erwise, the pastry will rise off the dish and then sink disastrously into the liquid. Our version comes out as a round, buttery, golden globe ascending like an airy balloon over the pungent, bubbly broth.

The Bread. Puff pastry is worth pursuing anytime and def-initely for this soup. Weigh the flour; do not gauge it by the cupful.

A chilly day is preferable for making puff pastry so that the butter keeps cold and manageable longer. Even on a cool day, you'll do yourself a favor if you chill the dough after every roll and fold. You can assemble good, easy-to-make puff pastry in about 1 hour. Your aim is to keep the butter-and-dough layers approximately the same temperature so that they roll evenly.

The Salad. The tomatoes should be fully red and ripe. If you can get them fresh and sweet from a garden, all the better.

Drink suggestion: red Burgundy wine

Truffle Soup

½ split chicken breast
water to cover chicken

MIREPOIX
2 T threaded and minced celery
2 T scraped and minced carrot
4 T destemmed, peeled, and minced mushrooms
3.7 oz can of truffles, minced (reserve juice)

2 T virgin olive oil
1/16 t thyme
¼ C chicken broth
1 T white dry vermouth
1 C chicken broth
1 C light strength beef bouillon
salt to taste
black pepper, freshly ground
puff pastry for 4 (see p. 117)
1 egg, well beaten
kitchen string

1. Place one-half of a split chicken breast in a saucepan with water to cover it (approximately 2 cups). Over medium-low heat, let the chicken poach for 12 to 15 minutes. Remove the chicken breast and reserve the broth. Discard the skin and bones. Cut the meat into small dice with a sharp knife. Reserve the chicken meat.

2. Prepare the mirepoix. Finely mince the vegetables. Add the reserved truffle juice to the vegetables.

3. Heat the olive oil in a small skillet, and sauté the vegetables and thyme 2 to 3 minutes over medium-low heat.

4. Add ¼ cup of chicken broth and the vermouth. Cover the skillet, and let the mirepoix simmer for 10 to 12 minutes.

5. Combine the chicken broth and beef bouillon. Taste the broth for salt, and add it if necessary. Pass the pepper mill over the saucepan a few times. Heat the broth.

6. Ready four ovenproof dishes (ramekins) that are approximately 4 inches wide and 2 inches high with straight sides. (Individual soufflé dishes work well.)

7. Divide the mirepoix and chicken meat evenly between the dishes. Add ½ cup of hot broth to each dish.

8. See the following recipe for the puff pastry. Roll the pastry ¼ inch thick. Cut out four circles ½ inch larger than the top of each dish. Brush the rounds with beaten egg. Invert the rounds on top of the dishes, and secure them tightly with kitchen string.

9. Place the soup dishes on a baking sheet. Bake the soup with pastry in a preheated 500°F oven for 5 minutes. Reduce the heat to 350°F, and bake it another 5 minutes. Check periodically to see that the pastry isn't getting too brown.

10. Cut the strings, remove them from the dishes, and serve the soup at once.

Serves 4

Puff Pastry

½ lb sweet butter, room temperature
½ lb unbleached all-purpose flour (about 1½ C)
½ t salt
½ C cold water
1 egg, slightly beaten
kitchen string

1. With your hands, shape the butter into a single rectangle about 4 x 6 inches. Chill.
2. Weigh the flour. Place it in a bowl, and mix in the salt. Gradually stir in the water until the dough forms a ball.
3. On a flat surface, knead dough 3 to 4 minutes until smooth and slightly elastic. It should not be sticky.
4. Roll the dough into a large rectangle about 6 x 16 inches and about ¼ inch thick.
5. Place the butter in the center third of the dough, shaping the butter to fit with at least ½ inch short of the edge of the dough.
6. Fold the top third of the dough to cover the butter. Fold the bottom third of the dough over these layers. Seal the edges by pressing firmly with your fingers. Cover and chill for at least 15 minutes.
7. Follow this roll-and-fold step *four times*: place the dough on a floured surface with the seam-side of the dough to your right. Roll gently but steadily to the original size rectangle of 6 x 16 inches. Work quickly, being careful not to break the butter through the dough. If the butter breaks through the top or bottom, pat flour onto the butter and finish the step. Don't flatten the dough too hard or too fast. Fold the top third over the center. Fold the bottom third over these two layers. Cover and chill.
8. Now the pastry is ready to form. To use for this soup, roll the dough into a squarish shape large enough for four rounds at least 4½ inches in diameter. Place the top of the bowl on the

pastry, and cut the dough around it so that enough pastry will hang over the side of the dish to tie it with string.

9. Brush the pastry rounds with the egg. Place the soup in the dish (see soup instructions). Turn the pastry over as you center it over the top of the dish; the egg-brushed side is now underneath.

10. Fold the edge of the pastry around the dish, sealing in the soup. With the string, tie the pastry around the rim of the dish.

11. Bake on a lower shelf at 500°F for 5 minutes. Reduce the heat to 350°F and bake another 5 minutes or until golden.

12. Option: for a glaze, you can brush on a mixture of 1 egg beaten with 1 tablespoon of water immediately before you place the pastry in the oven.

Tomato Wedges with Green Goddess Dressing

2 *ripe tomatoes*
red leaf lettuce

DRESSING
2 *extra large egg yolks*
2 *anchovies*
1 *C destemmed, washed parsley (loosely packed)*
2 *chopped scallions (including the white stalk)*
2 *T tarragon vinegar*
½ *C olive oil*

1. Core the tomatoes, and slice them into wedges. Place artfully on a bed of lettuce.

2. For the dressing, place the yolks, anchovies, parsley, scallions, and vinegar in a blender or food processor. Whirl to blend.
3. While the blender is whirling at low speed, slowly pour in the oil. Pour the dressing over the tomato wedges and serve.

Serves 4

Lobster Bisque
Apple Mint Muffins
Belgian Endive Salad

The Soup. This is one soup for which there are few substitutes. The lobster should be fresh; and if you can't commit crustacicide, make sure your fish market boiled the lobster red that day.

The Bread. The delicate undertaste of mint takes these muffins to a dimension beyond what the moist apple already gives them. Use a tart apple like a Northern Spy; Granny Smiths work well, too. The secret of muffins, which are one of the swiftest breads you can make, is to mix the batter with restraint. Don't worry about the lumps; they're what help give muffins lift and lightness. This is one bread in which you don't want to stir and stretch the gluten, a reason that you mix the apples and mint first with the dry ingredients.

The Salad. With its slightly tartish flavor, Belgian endive is a white, 3- to 4-inch-long cylinder of compacted leaves tinged with pale green on the tips. Braised, it makes a delectable accompanying vegetable to an entrée; but if you use it fresh as a salad in this combination, it's equally tasty. Prosciutto has become nearly a generic term for a disquieting range of flavored hams. Authentic prosciutto offers a singular, mellow-aged taste, but our national laws on preservatives hinder finding it easily in this country. Quality delicatessens should have the closest choice.

Drink suggestion: sparkling cider

Lobster Bisque

    1 boiled lobster (1 to 1½ lb)
    1 T dry sherry
 1½ C fish broth
 1½ C chicken broth
    1 small stalk of celery, with leaves
    2 cloves
    3 peppercorns
    1 small bay leaf, crushed
    1 C dry white wine (Bordeaux works well)
       cheesecloth
    3 T sweet butter
 1½ T flour
    1 C milk
  ¾ C cream
    1 egg yolk, slightly beaten
       dash of freshly grated nutmeg
       salt and white pepper to taste

1. Remove all of the lobster meat from the tail and claws. Shred it into small pieces. Cover the meat with sherry, and set it aside.
2. Crush the lobster shells with a mallet or lobster crackers (nut crackers will do) and disjoint the legs, retaining as much of the juices as possible for the lobster broth. The softer leg pieces may be ground in a meat grinder and added to the kettle along with the fish broth, chicken broth, celery, cloves, peppercorns, bay leaf, and wine. (Omit the wine if you used it in your fish broth recipe.) Slowly boil all of these ingredients over medium heat for 30 minutes. If fish heads, tails, etc., are unavailable for a good fish broth, boil 1 cup of clam juice, 1 cup dry white

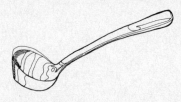

wine, a celery stalk, a sprig of parsley, a small peeled and chopped onion, and three peppercorns for 15 minutes; and strain.

3. Strain the lobster broth through a double layer of cheesecloth into a bowl.

4. In a medium-size saucepan, melt the butter and make a roux with flour. Slowly add the milk; cook the liquid over medium-low heat, stirring constantly. Do not boil.

5. Add 1½ cups of lobster broth and the lobster meat to the milk sauce. Continue cooking the soup over medium heat, stirring constantly.

6. Mix the cream with the egg yolk and add this to the bisque, making sure to whisk it into the soup. The bisque should never boil and should be the consistency of a heavy cream.

7. Season with a dash of nutmeg, salt, and pepper to taste.

Note: The lobster will be salty, so taste the bisque before adding salt.

Serves 4

Apple Mint Muffins

1 C chopped, peeled, and cored cooking apple
1 T minced fresh mint leaves
2 C unbleached all-purpose flour
2 t baking powder
½ t salt
3 T sugar
2 T melted sweet butter
1 C milk
1 extra large egg, well beaten

1. Prepare the apple and mint. Set aside.
2. Mix the flour, baking powder, salt, and sugar in a medium-size bowl.
3. Mix melted butter, milk, and egg in a small bowl.
4. Stir the apple and mint into the flour mixture.
5. Pour the milk mixture into the flour mixture, and lightly stir to moisten the ingredients. Do not overmix.
6. Spoon the dough into the oiled muffin tins two-thirds full.
7. Bake at 425°F for 15 to 20 minutes or until done.

Yields 6 to 8 muffins

Belgian Endive Salad

3 to 4 heads Belgian endive
3 very thin slices prosciutto
¼ C walnut pieces

DRESSING
4 T walnut oil
1½ t balsamic vinegar
salt to taste

1. Slice away the stem part of the endive; then carefully peel the leaves free, and place them artfully in a salad bowl.
2. Tear prosciutto into bite-size pieces, and scatter them over the endive.
3. Sprinkle walnuts over the endive and prosciutto.
4. For the dressing, mix the oil and vinegar. Salt to taste. Whisk to blend, and pour over the salad.

Serves 4

Sateh Soup
Poppadums
Tropical Fruit Salad

The Soup. Sateh is a common Indonesian dish. The marinated meats can include pork and veal. Chicken broth transforms the traditional peanut-coconut sauce into a soup. You may use more of the harrisa, but don't tempt fate—it is explosively HOT. Sateh calls for several ingredients that you can find in an Indian market or specialty food shop. It takes quite a few steps to prepare. However, this soup buys a taste passage to Indonesia bound to please dinner guests.

The Bread. Chick pea flour is available at most natural foods stores; you can also use lentil flour in Poppadums, an East Indian bread. Although traditionally served with curries, as crackly accompaniments they fit this and similar soups, too.

The Salad. This is an orange-hued salad; but if you wish a bolder mix of colors, it can easily take on a sliced banana and kiwi. The smooth, mellow taste of the mango is always a delight and fits with its taste cousin, the papaya. Meanwhile, the ugli, a loose-skinned, grapefruit-sized "orange" without the grapefruit tartness (it's related to the tangerine), brings the harmony of the mango and papaya into better perspective.

Drink suggestion: iced or hot orange pekoe tea

Sateh Soup

2 chicken breasts, split
3½ C water
½ t salt

MARINADE
2 cloves garlic, peeled, crushed, and minced
2 t curry
1 t coriander
2 t soybean paste (miso)
¼ C fresh lemon juice
2 scallions, thinly sliced (white part only)
   black pepper, freshly ground

1 C unsweetened coconut flakes
1 C boiling water
4 wood or metal skewers
1 T sweet butter
1 clove garlic, peeled, crushed, and minced
¼ C peeled and minced onion
1 t shrimp paste (trassie)
2 t brown sugar
½ C peanut butter
1 C coconut milk (from above flakes)
3 C chicken broth (from above)
   salt to taste
⅛ t harrisa (Indian chile sauce)

1. With poultry shears or a sharp knife, remove the bone and skin from the chicken breasts. Cut the meat into 1-inch pieces. Set it aside for the marinade. Place the chicken skin and bones in a medium-size saucepan with a lid. Add 3½ cups of water. Bring the water to a boil over high heat. Reduce the heat, and simmer the broth for 20 minutes. Strain out the chicken bones and skin, reserving the broth in a bowl. Stir in salt.

2. Mix all of the ingredients of the marinade together in a bowl large enough to hold the chicken pieces. Stir in the chicken so that the pieces are well coated with marinade. Cover the bowl with a plate or wrap, and set it aside for 1 hour.

3. Place the coconut flakes in a teapot. Add the boiling water. Stir once, and let the coconut steep for 20 minutes. Strain off 1 cup of coconut milk, which you will use later.

4. Remove the chicken from the marinade and place it on paper towels, dabbing off the marinade. Thread the chicken onto the skewers—one skewer for each person.

5. Place the skewers on a grill or wire rack 4 inches from the preheated broilers. Broil the chicken 6 minutes on one side.

6. Melt the butter in a heavy skillet over low heat. Add the minced garlic and minced onion, and cover the skillet 3 to 4 minutes or until the onion is limp.

7. Add the shrimp paste and brown sugar to the onion. Stir and cook it another minute or so.

8. Turn the heat to medium. Add the peanut butter and whisk as it bubbles, slowly pouring in the coconut milk until you have used all of the milk and the mixture is smooth. Remove the skillet from the burner.

9. Turn the chicken skewers over, and broil the chicken on the other side for 4 minutes.

10. Return the peanut sauce to low heat. Slowly whisk in the 3 cups of chicken broth. Taste for salt. Add the harissa.

11. Reheat the soup to a boil, but do not overheat it because the peanut butter may separate. Serve the skewers one to each person, and eat the chicken in the soup or separately. If the skewers are metal, the cook must wear a potholder to fork the chicken off the skewers for each guest.

Serves 4

Poppadums

½ C chick pea flour
¼ C rice flour
½ t (scant) salt
1 T peanut oil
3 T water
  peanut oil

1. In a medium-size bowl, mix the chick pea flour, rice flour, and salt.
2. Form a hollow in the center of the mixture, and pour in the oil. Blend with a wooden spoon.
3. Add the water by the tablespoon, and mix until a solid dough forms.
4. Divide into six equal parts. Form a ball with each part, flatten with your hand, and place on a flat, floured surface. Roll as thinly as you can; the rounds should be translucent. Cut out a 5-inch circle (an overturned dish approximately this size works well as a guide). Transfer the rounds to a baking sheet, and let dry (about 2 hours).
5. Fry the circles in an iron skillet with ¼ inch of hot peanut oil. Turn over nearly at once. The poppadums will curl and bubble. When done, transfer them to an absorbent paper towel. At this point, you can serve them, or place them on a baking sheet and crisp them up again under a broiler.

Yields 6 poppadums

Tropical Fruit Salad

1 mango
1 papaya
1 ugli

DRESSING
3 T unflavored yogurt
¼ t coriander
½ t honey
1 t lemon juice

1. Peel the mango, and cut sections of the fruit away from the large seed. Cut into bite-size pieces, and place in a medium-size mixing bowl.
2. Cut the papaya into quarters, and scrape away the seeds. Cut sections of the fruit away from the skin. Cut the fruit into bite-size pieces, and add to the mango.
3. Peel and section the ugli. Scrape away any residue skin pulp. Cut the sections into bite-size pieces, and add to the other fruit.
4. For the dressing, blend the yogurt, coriander, honey, and lemon juice. Pour over the fruit, and stir to coat. Serve in fruit cups or on a bed of tender greens.

Serves 4 to 6

Melon Mango Soup (Cold)
Cream Rolls
Old-fashioned Potato Salad

The Soup. You can buy brut champagne in a split. This soup bubbles cool and frothy on a hot, sultry summer day. The colors of orange melon and mango dotted with pale lime-green honeydew are easy on the eyes under a blazing sun. The spritz of the champagne lends just enough sparkle to enliven lazy diners.

The Bread. These take surprisingly little time to make for such light, subtle-tasting yeast rolls. The cream takes the place of shortening and adds a mellow undertaste. Served warm with melting sweet butter on them, they're a rich accompaniment. With red raspberry jam, they're luscious alone anytime day or night.

The Salad. Two potato salad camps predominate—one likes it dry, the other likes it moist. Marinating the salad in broth produces the latter. This version is a basic moist recipe to which you can add extra vegetables, such as pimientos and sweet red peppers, for color and taste.

Drink suggestion: brut champagne

Melon Mango Soup (Cold)

3 C diced ripe cantaloupe
1½ to 2 C peeled and sliced (from the seed) ripe mango
2 T fresh lime juice
1 C brut champagne or dry sparkling white wine
1 C small honeydew melon balls

1. Purée the cantaloupe and mango in a blender or a food processor. (You can extract the juice from the mango seed by squeezing the pulpy seed with clean hands.)
2. Add the lime juice to the puréed fruit, and blend it in.
3. Place the soup in a covered container, and refrigerate it for at least 2 hours. (Chilling will take less time if all of the ingredients are initially cold.)
4. Just before serving the soup, uncork the champagne or sparkling wine and pour it into the soup.
5. Garnish each portion with a few honeydew melon balls.

Serves 4

Cream Rolls

1½ t yeast
2 T warm water
¼ t (scant) salt
  pinch of sugar
1 extra large egg, slightly beaten
½ C heavy cream
1½ to 1¾ C unbleached all-purpose flour
  sweet butter
  cream

1. Dissolve the yeast in the water. Stir in the salt and sugar.
2. Combine the egg and cream. Blend these into the yeast mixture.
3. Mix in 1 cup of the flour before adding ½ cup more. Place on a flat surface and knead until smooth, adding flour to prevent sticking.
4. Form the dough into a cylinder, and with a knife mark eight equal sections. Cut off the pieces, and, by continuously tucking the dough inside the bottom, form smooth ball shapes.
5. Place the rolls in an 8-inch cake pan greased with sweet butter. Seven rolls will fit around one in the center. Cover with a cloth, and let rise in a warm place for 45 to 60 minutes or until doubled in bulk (don't let them overrise).
6. Brush the tops with cream.
7. Bake at 400°F for 15 minutes or until golden. Serve warm.

Yields 8 rolls

Old-fashioned Potato Salad

8 to 10 *medium-size new potatoes*
1 *whole medium-size onion, diced*
1 *T fresh minced chives*
1½ *C salted chicken broth*
2 *stalks celery, washed and threaded*
3 *hard-boiled eggs, peeled and chopped*
2 *diced whole crisp kosher dill pickles*
3 *T mayonnaise*
black pepper, freshly ground
salt to taste

1. In a large saucepan, cover the potatoes with cold water. Bring to a boil, and reduce the heat to a slow boil. Cook until a knife pierces the potatoes. They shouldn't break apart but be firm.
2. Let the potatoes cool in a colander to room temperature.
3. Peel the potatoes, and cube into a large bowl or casserole that you can cover.
4. Add the onions, chives, and broth; and mix well.
5. Cover and refrigerate (may be refrigerated overnight).
6. Add the celery, peeled and chopped eggs, pickles, and mayonnaise. Mix well.
7. Taste and add salt and pepper.

Serves 8 to 10

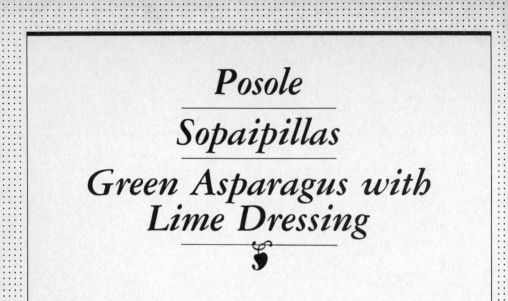

Posole

Sopaipillas

Green Asparagus with Lime Dressing

The Soup. This cook first had posole at a small bodega in San Miguel de Allende, Mexico. The recipe went something like this: "Take the cracked corn and boil it with a pig's head, hocks, and tomatoes for 3 hours." The corn wouldn't soften. After 3 hours, only a squirrel could have eaten it. "But you must boil it first in lye," a Mexican cook said. "Then each kernel must be hulled." One day we discovered prepared posole, cracked corn that has been presoaked and hulled. A New York friend remembers posole as samp, a typical Long Island dish boiled with salt pork for hours on end. Take some advice: buy the prepared posole or cooked canned whole hominy. If you use canned hominy, reduce the cooking time by 1 hour.

The Bread. These "little pillow" breads are the most attractive when made precisely and handled delicately to preserve their shape, and they're best served warm. A traditional way to serve them in the Southwest is to cut off a corner of the steam-filled pouch and slip some honeybutter inside.

The Salad. One of the first signs of spring is wild asparagus along roadsides and in fields. These tender, thin stalks grow to salad size in a few days and are delectable. If you miss the wild ones, asparagus found at the market still make this a divine salad.

Drink suggestion: margaritas

Posole

2 C prepared posole (2 C canned whole hominy may be substituted)
  water to cover
1 large chicken breast
1 lb country-style pork loin ribs
1 fresh pork hock (unsmoked)
1 beef marrow bone
8 C cold water
2 T peeled and minced onion
2 t salt
2 C peeled whole tomatoes, with juice
2 cloves garlic, peeled, crushed, and minced
1 T green jalapeño chile sauce
1 T chile powder
  salt to taste
¼ t imported oregano

GARNISH
½ C peeled chopped onion
½ C chopped green pepper

1 C shredded lettuce

1. (If you're using canned hominy, start with step 3.) In a large
   kettle, cover the prepared posole with water. Bring the water
   to a boil, and boil the posole for 5 minutes. Cover the kettle.
   Take it off the burner, and let it sit overnight.
2. Drain the posole. Add fresh water to cover it, and cook it 1½
   to 2 hours or until the kernels explode like popcorn.
3. Place the next seven ingredients in a large soup kettle. Bring
   them to a boil. Reduce the heat, and boil the soup slowly for
   2 hours.
4. After 2 hours, remove the marrow from the beef bone. Cut bite-
   size pieces of meat from the other bones. Discard the bones and
   return the chicken, pork, and marrow to the soup.
5. Add the posole (or canned hominy), tomatoes, garlic, chile sauce

and powder, extra salt to taste, and oregano. Cook the posole 30 minutes more.

6. Serve posole with small pottery bowls containing the garnish on the side.

Serves 4 to 6

Sopaipillas

> 1 C unbleached all-purpose flour
> 1 t baking powder
> ¼ t salt
> 1 T sweet butter
> ⅓ C water
> corn oil

1. Mix the flour, baking powder, and salt.
2. Cut in the butter. Stir in the water.
3. Place on a flat surface, and knead a few minutes until smooth and elastic. Cover with a cloth, and let rest 15 to 20 minutes.
4. With a rolling pin, flatten the dough into a rectangle measuring 6 x 12 inches and slightly less than ⅛ inch thick. Cut away excess dough to make straight edges.
5. With a ruler, measure 3-inch squares. Cut them exactly.
6. Fry the squares briefly in hot oil (365°F) until they expand like balloons. Turn over, and fry until they are golden on both sides.
7. Remove with a slotted spoon or a deep-fry basket, and place them on an absorbent paper towel. Serve immediately.

Yields 8 sopaipillas

Green Asparagus with Lime Dressing

24 to 32 very thin asparagus spears
Bibb lettuce

DRESSING
3 T walnut oil
1½ t fresh lime juice
salt to taste

1. Depending on the texture of the spears, cut off the bottom third or half. Steam the tops until firm but tender (about 8 to 10 minutes). Plunge them into cold water. Dry and place on a bed of lettuce.
2. For the dressing, mix the oil, lime juice, and salt. Pour over the salad and serve.

Serves 4

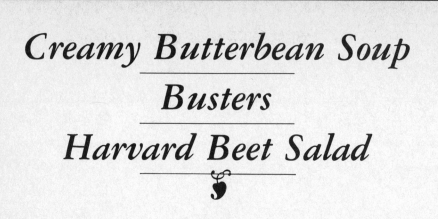

Creamy Butterbean Soup
Busters
Harvard Beet Salad

The Soup. Butterbeans are large, yellow lima beans high in protein and vitamin A, at the top of the scale in potassium, and well endowed with calcium and phosphorus. You may want to pass the tomatoes through a food mill to remove the seeds before you purée them. You can easily double or triple this recipe for a large crowd. Butterbean soup provides a quick, hot, nourishing midday lunch.

The Bread. Associated with Australia, busters make good soup accompaniments anywhere. This version is very cheesy and spicy; you can lighten them by using a mild cheddar and reducing the amount of cayenne. Busters double in height with baking; and they become addictive, so a whole basketful is always appropriate.

The Salad. Usually served as a hot vegetable, these sweet-and-sour beets, when chilled, make an invigorating salad. Dishes garnished with shredded egg are often called mimosa, but any way you look at the bright yellow yolk against the royal purple beets, this is a rich-tasting combination.

Drink suggestion: egg cream

Creamy Butterbean Soup

2 slices of lean bacon, diced
1 t virgin olive oil
1 C peeled whole tomatoes, with juice
1 T peeled and grated onion, with juice
1 can butterbeans (15 oz), drained
2 C chicken broth

1. Over medium heat, sauté the bacon in olive oil in a medium-size skillet.
2. Pass the tomatoes through a food mill or strainer to extract the seeds.
3. If there is more than 1 teaspoon of fat rendered from the bacon, pour it off.
4. Add the grated onion to the fat, and lower the heat to medium-low. Cook the onions 2 to 3 minutes.
5. Add tomatoes, and simmer them while preparing the butterbeans.
6. Remove any loose skins from the beans. The skins are tough and will not blend easily if they are detached from the bean.
7. Place the beans and 1 cup of chicken broth in a blender or food processor, and blend them well at least 2 minutes.
8. Add the onion-tomato-bacon mixture, and continue to blend them well for 2 minutes.
9. Place the blended mixture in a medium-size soup kettle, and heat the soup over medium heat. Add the remaining cup of chicken broth, stir, and heat the soup until it reaches the boiling point. Serve.

Serves 4

Busters

4 T sweet butter
1 C unbleached all-purpose flour
1½ C grated Romano (about 3 oz)
⅛ t (scant) cayenne red pepper
¼ C water

1. Rub the butter into the flour until it's dispersed into small pieces.
2. Mix in the cheese.
3. Add the cayenne.
4. Gradually stir in the water to form a ball of dough. With your hands, very briefly knead the dough to make it uniform.
5. On a floured flat surface, roll the dough into a circle ¼ inch thick. Cut out the busters with a 2-inch biscuit cutter. Place the busters on an oiled baking sheet.
6. Pierce the top of each buster with the tines of a fork, making a uniform pattern.
7. Bake at 450°F for 6 to 8 minutes or until lightly toasted.

Yields 20 busters

Harvard Beet Salad

4 medium-size beets, cooked and peeled

DRESSING
¼ C sugar
¼ t salt
1 t cornstarch

⅛ t grated fresh gingerroot
¼ C cider vinegar
1 T sweet butter

shredded lettuce
yolk of 1 hard-boiled egg

1. Slice the beets ¼ inch thick in rounds, and set aside.
2. In a small saucepan, combine the sugar, salt, cornstarch, gingerroot, vinegar, and butter. Place over medium-high heat and cook until thickened, stirring continuously.
3. Add the beets to the sauce, and coat thoroughly.
4. Remove the beets with a slotted spoon, and arrange in overlapping slices on the lettuce. Pour the remaining sauce over each of the servings. Chill.
5. Meanwhile, finely grate the yolk onto a plate and reserve. Immediately before serving, sprinkle the yolk lightly over the beets.

Serves 4

Wild Rice Mushroom Soup
Potato Bread
Wilted Spinach Salad

The Soup. Native Americans gather wild rice in northern Minnesota, Wisconsin, and Michigan. Wild rice isn't really a rice at all, but a wild grass. You can't substitute brown or white rice for the unique, crunchy grains and dark, nutty flavor of wild rice. Cook wild rice separately because the cooking water has quite an acrid taste. This soup provides a welcome change from the ubiquitous cream of mushroom soup. Of course, the best combination would be wild rice and wild mushrooms; however, we suggest this only if you are a mushroom expert with thorough knowledge of the delicacies of the woods.

The Bread. This bread has more potato flavor than actual potato, which keeps the loaf light tasting but still full-bodied and moist. You'll find the dough very pliable and easy to knead. Instead of boiling a potato, you can use potato starch for similar results, although you'll need to increase the amount of water. The crust on this is the old-fashioned chewy kind—and a good crust is one of the prized advantages of homemade bread.

The Salad. Choice, young, tender spinach leaves are essential for this salad. To vary this theme for a vegetable side dish, "wilt" the spinach in the skillet with the sauce; but if you like crisper greens, stick to the suggestions as given.

Drink suggestion: fresh carrot juice

Wild Rice Mushroom Soup

3 T sweet butter
12 oz mushrooms
⅛ t basil
⅛ t oregano
⅛ t thyme
2 T peeled and grated onion, with juice
½ C wild rice
   water to cover
6 C beef broth
2 T lemon juice
   lemon slices
   Romano or Parmesan cheese, freshly grated

1. Melt the butter in a large soup kettle over medium heat.
2. Peel the mushrooms, and cut off the woody part of the stems. (Washed mushrooms don't sauté as well as peeled mushrooms.) Sauté them in the butter.
3. Add basil, oregano, thyme, and grated onion with juice. Cover the kettle, and let the mushrooms sweat over medium-low heat for about 10 minutes or until they are fairly soft and limp.
4. Wash the wild rice. Place it in a medium-size saucepan, and cover the rice with 3 inches of cold water. Bring it to a boil. Reduce the heat to low, and simmer the rice, covered, for 30 minutes.
5. Add the beef broth to the mushrooms. (You may also use half veal or chicken stock.) Simmer them, covered, for 30 minutes.
6. Drain the cooked rice, and add it to the soup.
7. Add the lemon juice. Top each serving with a slice of lemon. Place a bowl of Parmesan cheese on the table.

Serves 4

Potato Bread

⅓ C mashed cooked potato
1 C potato water
1 T yeast
   pinch of sugar
1½ t salt
1 T oil
3¼ C unbleached all-purpose flour

1. In a mixing bowl, stir the mashed potato into the reserved water used to boil the potato. If the water is cool, warm it slightly.
2. Sprinkle yeast over the potato water mixture to dissolve.
3. Add the sugar, salt, and oil.
4. Beat in nearly all the flour. Place the dough on a flat surface and knead for 8 to 10 minutes, adding flour to prevent sticking. Place dough in an oiled bowl, turn over so the top is coated with oil, cover with a cloth, and let rise in a warm spot until doubled in bulk (about 1½ hours).
5. Punch down dough, and remove from the bowl. With your hands, tuck the dough continuously underneath itself to make a smooth top. Shape into an oblong, and place it in an oiled bread pan. Cover and let rise until doubled in bulk (about 1 hour).
6. Bake at 400°F for 25 to 30 minutes or until done. Brush with sweet butter, and cool on a wire rack.

Yields 1 loaf

Wilted Spinach Salad

4 C destemmed and shredded young spinach leaves
2 hard-boiled eggs, halved

DRESSING
4 rashers of lean bacon
¼ C diced onion
¼ C cider vinegar
1½ t sugar

1. Prepare the spinach, and place in a warm serving bowl. Warm individual serving plates in the oven. Prepare the eggs, and set aside.
2. For the dressing, fry the bacon, reserving the fat. Remove the bacon to an absorbent paper towel to crisp. Finely crumble the bacon.
3. In the bacon drippings, sauté the onion until translucent. Add the vinegar, sugar, and bacon pieces. Turn on high heat.
4. To serve, pour the hot dressing over the spinach, and quickly toss before serving immediately on the warm plates. Top each serving with an egg half.

Serves 4

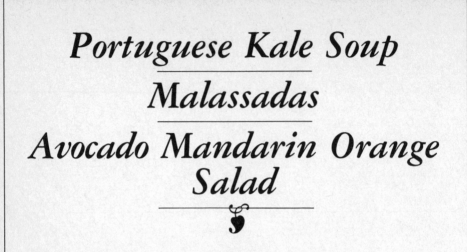

Portuguese Kale Soup
Malassadas
Avocado Mandarin Orange Salad

The Soup. Most recipes for Portuguese Kale Soup include potatoes, Portuguese sausage, and kale. If linguiça isn't available, you can substitute chorizo (hot Spanish pork sausage). Pinto beans, kidney beans, and chick peas often go into this soup. For women concerned with osteoporosis (brittle bones), Portuguese Kale Soup more than fills a woman's daily calcium requirement.

The Bread. Also called "flipper dough," this version of Portuguese fried dough is more manageable than the larger, thicker malassadas. Although you can eat them cold and fresh, eating them within the first five or ten minutes when they're still warm is better. These are like fritters. When forming them, don't fold the dough over itself; if you press and shape them on a flat surface, they tend to bubble on top when you fry them, adding unpredictable, appealing, free-form shapes.

The Salad. The smaller variety of avocado, which is at its peak when the fruit yields noticeably with a slight squeeze of your hand, offers the best flavor. Having patience with the ripening process brings its rewards because then the avocado is fully soft and buttery. The peeled avocado darkens with exposure to oxygen in the air, so either prepare this soon before serving or sprinkle the slices with lemon juice to retard the discoloration.

Drink suggestion: Portuguese vinho verde

Portuguese Kale Soup

4 T virgin olive oil
1 C peeled and finely diced onion
1 lb sliced linguiça Portuguese sausage
6 C water
2 C dry red wine
1 lb washed, destemmed, and finely chopped fresh kale
1 t salt
   dash of cayenne
1 T sugar
3 medium potatoes, peeled and diced
1 lb rinsed and drained butterbeans

1. Heat the olive oil in a large, heavy kettle.
2. Add the onions, and sauté them 2 to 3 minutes. Cover and sweat onions 5 to 8 minutes or until they're limp.
3. Add the linguiça Portuguese sausage to the onions, and sauté it 2 to 3 minutes.
4. Add the water, wine, kale, salt, cayenne, and sugar to the soup kettle.
5. Cover the soup, and simmer it over medium heat for 1 hour.
6. Add the potatoes, and continue cooking the soup for 15 minutes.
7. Add the beans, and simmer the soup another 15 minutes. Check to see if more liquid is needed. The consistency should be like a thin stew.

Serves 8

Malassadas

1 T yeast
¼ C warm water
½ C milk
¼ C sweet butter
¼ C sugar
½ t salt
1 extra large egg, slightly beaten
3 C unbleached all-purpose flour
confectioners' sugar

1. Dissolve the yeast in the water.
2. In a small saucepan, combine the milk, butter, sugar, and salt. Heat and stir to dissolve the solids. Remove from the heat, and cool to lukewarm.
3. Combine the cooled milk mixture with the yeast mixture. Stir in the egg.
4. Mix in the flour. Place the dough on a flat surface, and knead 5 minutes or until smooth and elastic, adding only enough flour to prevent sticking.
5. Place dough in an oiled bowl, turn over so the top is coated with the oil, cover with a cloth, and let rise in a warm spot until doubled in bulk (about 1 hour).
6. Punch down dough, and form into a cylinder on a flat surface. Break off large, plum-size pieces; and, by pressing and stretching the dough between your fingers, form a rectangle about 5 x 3 inches and less than ¼ inch thick.
7. Deep fry in vegetable oil heated to 375°F until golden brown on each side (about 15 seconds). Remove from the oil; place on a wire rack and, while still warm, sprinkle the malassadas with confectioners' sugar.

Yields 12 malassadas

Avocado Mandarin Orange Salad

1 avocado, peeled
shredded lettuce
½ C drained mandarin oranges

DRESSING
4 T unflavored yogurt
2 t honey
⅛ t coriander

1. Slice the length of the avocado in half, remove the seed, and slice each half into eight lengths. Arrange the slices in a row on the lettuce, four to a serving.
2. Insert two orange sections between each avocado slice.
3. For the dressing, mix the yogurt, honey, and coriander. Drape the dressing diagonally across the avocado and oranges.

Serves 4

Winter Melon Soup

Cha Siew Bao

Steamed Broccoli with Tahini Dressing

The Soup. The Chinese partake of clear soups for breakfast, lunch, and dinner. In the States, winter melon usually appears in Chinese markets from November through February. It grows as large as watermelon, and you can recognize it by its dark green shell covered with a fine white powder that resembles winter frost. The Chinese carve the shell, depicting intricate scenes; then they serve the soup in the rind. Winter melon has little taste, yet the translucent bits lend an appealing texture buoyed up by the headier garlic, scallion, and ginger flavors. Many recipes for winter melon soup call for chicken breast; however, the breast tends to get tough and stringy with boiling. Chicken quarters make a good, strong broth; in addition, the meat remains succulent and tender.

The Bread. Fill these steamed buns with chicken, fish, or vegetables. The steaming lightens and thickens the dough as well as glistens the surface a shiny white. Being bite-size and delicious, they're just right for appetizers.

The Salad. Tahini is sesame seeds ground to a paste; on opening the can, recombine the tahini with its natural oil, which separates. Simply stir until smooth. Along with chick peas, tahini is one of the basic ingredients to hummus, a popular Middle Eastern dish.

Drink suggestion: warm rice wine

Winter Melon Soup

2 chicken quarters (leg plus thigh)
6 C water
1 t salt
4 dried black mushrooms
1 C warm water
4 C peeled and cubed winter melon (approximately
   a 3-lb slice of melon)
1 clove garlic, peeled, crushed, and minced
1 t sugar
1 T light soy sauce
2 t peanut oil
2 scallions (white part and 2 inches of green part,
   cut into ½-inch rounds)
1 slice gingerroot, peeled and minced

1. Place the chicken quarters in a soup kettle with the water, and bring it to a boil. Cover, reduce the heat, and simmer the broth for 25 minutes. Add salt.
2. Soak the dried mushrooms in 1 cup of warm water. Weight them down with a small saucer so that they're completely immersed. Soak them for 15 minutes.
3. While soaking the mushrooms, prepare the melon.
4. Drain the mushrooms, and squeeze out the excess water. Slice each mushroom into slivers from the stem. The stems are tough, so be sure to discard them.
5. Remove the chicken from the broth, and let it cool.
6. Mix the garlic, sugar, and soy sauce in a bowl.
7. Remove the skin from the chicken, and shred off bite-size pieces of the meat. Place 1 cup of the chicken meat in the bowl with the soy sauce marinade. Set it aside for 15 minutes.
8. Add the winter melon and mushrooms to the broth. Return the broth to a boil; then lower the heat, cover, and cook the soup at a slow boil for 30 minutes or until the melon turns translucent.
9. Heat the peanut oil in a wok or a small skillet. Sauté the

scallions and gingerroot in the hot oil for 1 to 2 minutes. Pour off the excess oil. Add the chicken soy sauce mixture, and swish it around to clean the skillet; then add the chicken soy sauce mixture to the broth.

10. Serve Winter Melon Soup in Chinese rice bowls or lacquered bowls. These best show off the translucent melon.

Serves 6

Cha Siew Bao

1 T yeast
½ C warm water
¼ t salt
1 C unbleached all-purpose flour

FILLING
3 scallions, minced (white part only)
½ t grated fresh ginger
2 T peanut oil
½ lb ground pork sausage

1. For the buns, dissolve the yeast in the water. Stir in the salt, and mix in the flour.
2. On a flat surface, knead dough 5 minutes or until smooth and elastic.
3. Place dough in an oiled dish, turn over so the top is coated with oil, cover with a cloth, and let rise in a warm spot for 1 hour.
4. For the filling, sauté the scallions and ginger in the oil.
5. Add the sausage and brown well, mashing the meat into small pieces. Remove from the heat, and set aside.
6. To assemble, punch down the dough and place on a flat surface. Break off egg-size pieces, and pat into 3-inch circles.

7. Place 1 tablespoon of pork mixture in the center of each circle. Bring two opposite dough edges over the mixture and seal. Cut off excess dough from the remaining sides, leaving enough to seal in the pork. Gently seal the sides and tuck under along the seam, forming miniature loaves.
8. Cover and let rise for 15 to 20 minutes.
9. Over boiling water, place the buns well apart in a steamer basket to allow for expansion. Cover and steam for 5 to 10 minutes or until the surface glistens and is firm to the touch. Serve warm.

Yields 10 to 12 buns

Steamed Broccoli with Tahini Dressing

fresh broccoli for four
vinegar water

DRESSING
garlic clove tip, crushed and minced
1½ *T fresh lemon juice*
2 *T tahini*
⅛ *t salt*
1 *T chopped parsley*
2 *t olive oil*

Boston lettuce

1. Prepare the broccoli by slicing the florets from the stems and soaking them for 10 minutes in vinegar water. Drain.
2. Steam the broccoli for 8 to 10 minutes or until done.

3. Immediately plunge the broccoli into cold water. Drain and air dry.
4. For the dressing, mix the garlic, lemon juice, tahini, salt, parsley, and oil. The dressing will be thick.
5. To serve, place the broccoli in a fan shape on a single bed of lettuce. Drape the dressing over part of the broccoli.

Serves 4

Parsley Soup (Cold)

Croissants

Salade Niçoise

The Soup. Italian parsley is flat-leafed and has a distinctive pungent flavor. Curly parsley ordinarily is used for garnishes. Grow both in the garden or a windowbox so that they are absolutely fresh.

The Bread. Homemade fresh croissants with their puffy, crisp, dark brown glaze and flaky butter-laden layers inside are qualitative leaps beyond the factory versions. No denying it, croissants take some feel for baking. On the other hand, they are nowhere near as difficult as their mythology engenders.

The Salad. Fresh tuna offers a far better focused taste than canned. Boil the potatoes and beans in lightly salted water, and be gingerly in adding salt to the marinade and dressing, because the olives and anchovies provide their own. The brilliant colors in this salad come from the freshest, choicest vegetables you can find.

Drink suggestion: Montrachet wine

Parsley Soup (Cold)

 2 T sweet butter
 3 leeks, washed well and thinly sliced (white part only)
 ¼ C chicken broth
 ¾ C dry white wine
 1½ C peeled and cubed potatoes
 4¾ C chicken broth
    salt and white pepper to taste
 1 C destemmed and finely minced Italian parsley
 1 C heavy cream

1. Melt butter in a heavy soup kettle over low heat.
2. Add the leeks and ¼ cup of chicken broth. Sweat the leeks in the broth over low heat, covered, until they are limp (approximately 5 to 8 minutes).
3. Add the wine, potatoes, chicken broth, salt, and white pepper according to preference. (If the chicken broth is heavily salted, adding more salt will be unnecessary.)
4. Cover the kettle, and simmer the soup over medium heat for 30 minutes.
5. Add the parsley, and simmer it 5 more minutes.
6. Transfer the soup to the blender in batches, and purée each batch 2 minutes. Pour the soup into a large pitcher.
7. Stir in the cream.
8. Refrigerate the Parsley Soup at least 2 hours or until it is well chilled, then pour it into individual bowls.

Serves 4

Croissants

1 T yeast
¼ C warm water
1 T sugar
½ t salt
½ C lukewarm milk
2¼ C unbleached all-purpose flour
½ lb sweet butter, room temperature

GLAZE
1 egg yolk
1 T heavy cream

1. Dissolve the yeast in the water.
2. Add the sugar, salt, and milk.
3. Beat in the flour. Place dough on a flat surface, and knead 8 to 10 minutes until smooth and elastic, adding flour to prevent sticking.
4. Place dough in an oiled bowl, turn over so the top is coated with oil, cover with a cloth, and let rise in a warm spot until doubled in bulk (about 1½ hours).
5. Punch down dough, and roll out to a 14 x 10-inch rectangle. Slice the butter, and spread evenly on the top two-thirds of the dough to within 1 inch of the edges.
6. Fold the botton third over the middle third. Fold the top third over the other two. Set on a plate, cover with a cloth, and chill for 10 minutes or until the butter is firm but not hard.
7. Sprinkle flour on a flat working surface to prevent sticking. Roll the dough to a 14 x 10-inch rectangle again. Work fast without damaging the layers of dough. Fold in thirds again in the original way, and turn the dough a quarter turn so that you'll be rolling it from a different edge. Repeat this procedure of rolling, folding, and turning in the same direction *three* times. It's usually better to chill the dough 10 to 15 minutes between each rolling so that the butter remains firm and won't seep through the dough layers.

8. To shape, roll out the dough to an 18 x 12-inch rectangle. Trim the edges to meet these dimensions. With a ruler, mark off six 6-inch squares and cut with a sharp knife.

9. Roll each square on the diagonal—from point to point. End with the point on the bottom of the croissant. Bend the ends inward to form a U-shaped croissant.

10. Place on two lightly oiled baking sheets, and let set at room temperature for 30 minutes.

11. For the glaze, mix the egg yolk and cream. Brush onto the croissants.

12. Bake at 450°F for 10 minutes. Reduce the temperature to 350°F, and continue to bake for 15 minutes or until done.

Yields 6 croissants

Salade Niçoise

⅓ lb fresh tuna
2 C reconstituted dry milk
  oil
2 C peeled and boiled new potatoes (about 4 small potatoes)
1 C fresh, young, thin, boiled green beans (snapped into 1-inch sections)
2 T olive oil
2 t balsamic vinegar
  salt to taste
1 large tomato
1 T chopped parsley
9 Greek olives
1 t capers
1 (2 oz) can anchovy fillets

DRESSING
3 T *virgin olive oil*
1 T *balsamic vinegar*
2 t *chopped fresh chives*
   salt and pepper to taste

1. Poach the tuna 8 to 10 minutes (depending on the thickness of the cut) in the milk. Coat the tuna with oil, and set aside.
2. Cube the potatoes to bite-size. Combine with the beans in a large mixing bowl. Mix oil, vinegar, and salt; and coat the potatoes and beans. Place in the bottom of the serving bowl.
3. Cut the tomato to bite-size wedges (about 12 to 14), and place around the edge of the bowl. Sprinkle parsley on the tomatoes.
4. Space olives artfully near the tomatoes, and sprinkle the capers over the entire salad.
5. Separate the tuna into sections, and place in a circle toward the center of the salad. Drape the anchovies across the top. Cover the salad, and chill.
6. For the dressing, mix the oil, vinegar, chives, salt, and pepper and pour over the salad. Toss the salad with wooden spoons, and serve.

Serves 4

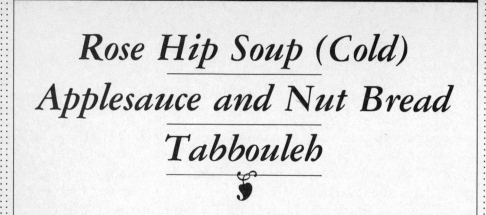

Rose Hip Soup (Cold)
Applesauce and Nut Bread
Tabbouleh

The Soup. Contrary to what you might think, rose hips aren't the anatomy of a lovely lady extolled by Victorian poetry. They are the fruit of the rose, and you can find dried rose hips in most health food stores. They come whole, like little dried cherries, and have a dark, marly odor. This is a fruit soup that you can serve cold or hot. In the winter it is a good choice for the flu season because it excels in vitamin C. It will also keep guests guessing.

The Bread. Tart apples make the best sauce, and choices abound on seasoning applesauce. Try a combination of allspice and mace, brown sugar, and maybe a dash of red wine. As for this quick bread, its rich, multicolored texture is moist and comforting. Serve thick slices warm with dissolving sweet butter on top—the bread nearly melts in your mouth.

The Salad. Bulgur is slightly toasted cracked wheat. When steeped, it softens into a light, nutty-tasting grain. For tabbouleh, you can soften the bulgur with plain boiling water, but we find that chicken broth gives it a richer taste. This recipe is a restrained rendition of the Middle Eastern classic. Choice, fresh ingredients are important. Destemming the mint and parsley eliminates any bitterness. If you can, serve this outdoors. Perfect for summer.

Drink suggestion: mineral water

Rose Hip Soup (Cold)

2 C dried rose hips
6 C cold water, divided
¼ C lemon juice
½ C honey
½ C chopped Turkish apricots
2 T arrowroot
½ C water
½ C heavy cream, whipped
   nutmeg, freshly grated

1. Place the rose hips in a saucepan having a lid. Cover them with water (approximately 3 cups). Bring them to a boil over high heat for 1 minute. Cover them, and turn off the heat. Let the rose hips soak overnight. Don't remove the lid.
2. When they're ready to use, bring them to a boil with the remaining 3 cups of water. Reduce the heat, cover them, and let them simmer for 45 minutes.
3. Strain the liquid into a bowl, and discard the rose hips. You will have approximately 4½ cups of rose hip broth.
4. Place the broth in a saucepan with the lemon juice, honey, Turkish apricots, and arrowroot that you have dissolved in ½ cup of water.
5. Stir the soup as you bring it to a boil. Boil the soup for 10 minutes until it is thick and clear. Stir occasionally.
6. Serve with a dollop of whipped cream and a fillip of freshly grated nutmeg.

Serves 6

Applesauce and Nut Bread

2 C unbleached all-purpose flour
½ t salt
1 t baking soda
½ C brown sugar
1 extra large egg
½ C buttermilk
¼ C melted sweet butter
1 C sweetened and spiced applesauce
½ C chopped walnuts

1. Mix the flour, salt, and baking soda.
2. In a separate bowl, blend the brown sugar, egg, buttermilk, and melted butter.
3. Combine the sugar mixture with the flour mixture until well blended; the batter will be firm.
4. Stir in the applesauce until thoroughly blended.
5. Add the walnuts. Pour into a greased loaf pan.
6. Bake at 350°F for 1 hour or until done. Serve warm or cold.

Yields 1 loaf

Tabbouleh

2 C (scant) unsalted chicken broth
1 C bulgur
2 scallions, chopped (white stalks only)
⅓ C chopped fresh parsley

2 T chopped fresh mint leaves
1 C peeled and diced cucumber
2 T fresh lime juice
¾ C peeled and chopped tomato
1 t salt
2 T olive oil
   romaine lettuce
   yogurt

1. Bring the chicken broth to a boil. Pour the broth over the bulgur in a medium-size bowl. Cover tightly and let steep for about 1 hour or until cooled. The bulgur will absorb the broth and become light and soft.
2. Meanwhile, prepare the other vegetables. When the bulgur is at room temperature, fluff up with a fork; then mix all the ingredients except the oil and yogurt into the bulgur. Refrigerate for 2 hours.
3. Immediately before serving, blend the oil into the salad. Spoon onto beds of lettuce. Top with large dollops of unflavored yogurt.

Serves 4

Trout Soup Solianka
Pepper Pumpernickel
Caviar Salad

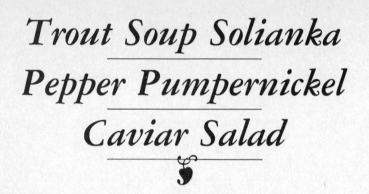

The Soup. Olives, capers and/or pickles, and lemon are usually common ingredients in this Russian fish soup. You can substitute salmon, sturgeon, and other oily types of fish for the trout. With the olives winking at you and the green capers and dill added, this is a highly colorful, festive soup.

The Bread. This sturdy, dark bread uses a detour from the familiar caraway seed flavor. The black pepper in this loaf charms the taste buds; if you disperse it sufficiently, it surfaces only as a backdrop. Although the pepper is discernible and lingers in your mouth, to someone other than the baker it's usually not quite identifiable. If you're leery about so much pepper, simply reduce the amount. Toasted, this bread makes good bacon, tomato, and lettuce sandwiches.

The Salad. Beluga caviar is roe from the female sturgeon that once flourished in the large rivers of this country but now is at no commercial level of population. So we must import this prized caviar. Other kinds of caviar are available from lumpfish, salmon, cod, and other fish. A traditional way of eating caviar is to very lightly butter the bread, place a sliver of salmon on top, spoon on some caviar, squeeze a little lemon juice on top, and garnish with the egg and parsley; then press the caviar to the top of your mouth.

Drink suggestion: chilled vodka

Trout Soup Solianka

4 trout (cleaned and filleted, with heads intact)
4 C cold water
1 C chicken broth
½ C clam juice

BOUQUET GARNI
½ bay leaf
3 sprigs parsley
1 slice onion
4 peppercorns, crushed
3 celery leaf sprigs
¼ t dried thyme (or 1 fresh sprig)
   cheesecloth
   kitchen thread

2 T sweet butter
½ C scraped and diced carrot
½ C peeled and diced onion
½ C threaded and diced celery
1 clove garlic, peeled and crushed
½ C peeled whole tomatoes, with juice
½ t salt
   black pepper, freshly ground
   trout pieces (from above)
2 T vodka
⅓ C fresh lemon juice (1 medium-size lemon)
1 T capers
1 t destemmed and minced parsley
2 t destemmed and minced fresh dill (dried dill may be substituted)
12 black pitted olives, coarsely chopped
   sour cream

1. Cut off the trout heads and small fins, and place them in a medium-size soup kettle with the cold water, chicken broth, and clam juice. Add the bouquet garni, which you place in the cheesecloth and tie with string. Cover the kettle, and simmer

the broth 20 to 25 minutes over medium heat. The fish broth will boil down to about 3¼ to 3½ cups.

2. Drain the broth through a strainer into a bowl, discarding the bouquet garni and trimmings. Reserve the fish broth.

3. In a saucepan, melt the butter over low heat and sauté the carrot, onion, celery, and garlic for 5 minutes.

4. Cover the vegetables, and simmer them for 10 minutes. Remove the garlic.

5. Heat the fish broth in a soup kettle. Add the sautéed vegetables and the tomatoes.

6. Season the soup with salt, pepper, vodka, and lemon juice. Bring it to a boil. Cover the kettle, and simmer the soup over medium heat for 10 minutes.

7. Cut each trout into three, then cut these pieces in half. Drop the trout into the soup, and boil it 2 to 3 minutes.

8. Take the solianka off the heat and add capers, parsley, dill, and olives.

9. Garnish each portion with a spoonful of sour cream, and serve another bowl of sour cream at the table.

Serves 6

Pepper Pumpernickel

> 2   T yeast
> 1   C freshly brewed espresso
> 1½ t salt
> 2   T corn oil
> 2   T unsulphured molasses
> 1¼ t freshly ground black pepper
> 1   C medium rye
> 1   C whole wheat
> 1   C unbleached all-purpose flour
>   cornmeal
>   sweet butter

1. Dissolve the yeast in warm (not hot) coffee.
2. Stir in the salt, oil, molasses, and pepper.
3. Beat in the rye, whole wheat, and unbleached flours. Place dough on a flat surface, and knead for 10 minutes.
4. Shape into a round loaf, and place on an oiled baking sheet sprinkled with cornmeal. Cover with a cloth, and let rise in a warm place until doubled in bulk (about 1½ hours).
5. Bake at 375°F for 30 minutes or until done. Brush with melted sweet butter.

Yields 1 loaf

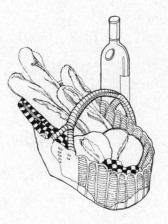

Caviar Salad

1 (2-oz) jar of caviar
¼ lb very thinly sliced smoked salmon
  sweet butter, softened and curled
1 fresh lemon, quartered
  Bibb lettuce leaves
1 hard-boiled egg, finely shredded
2 T destemmed, finely chopped Italian
  parsley
  black bread points, lightly toasted

1. Place the caviar, salmon, butter curls, and lemon side by side on the lettuce leaves.
2. Place the egg and parsley in separate bowls with serving spoons.
3. Keep the bread warm in a cloth-covered basket, and serve.

Serves 4

Fried Plantain Soup
Golden Saffron Buns
Deviled Eggs

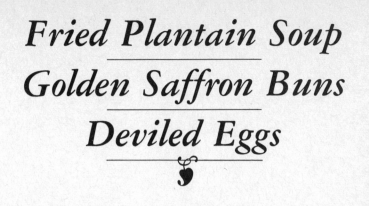

The Soup. Plantains look like chunky, rectangular-shaped bananas. They are sold green, so ripen them a few days on a windowsill until they become a chartreuse color. Peel the plantain well because the integument is bitter. Always cook plantains. The inner fruit reveals a delightful papaya color that turns golden when fried. Any brown slices will alter the taste, so be sure to discard them. Stir the soup when heating it; the plantain starch tends to coagulate on the bottom of the pan.

The Bread. Soft and spongy, these butter-colored rolls keep well if you have any left over, and are appealing anytime, breakfast included. You can bake them in two 8-inch cake pans, use one batch for this soup and salad, and freeze the second batch in the pan for easy thawing and warming later.

The Salad. You can make these mild eggs more "devilish" with a few more shakes of the very hot red pepper Tabasco sauce. These eggs, as you know, are perfect for picnics, too.

Drink suggestion: tropical fruit milkshake

Fried Plantain Soup

4½ C chicken or turkey broth
2 C plantains (2 whole plantains)
salted water to cover
safflower oil
½ t salt
½ C grated Monterey Jack cheese

1. Heat the chicken broth in a large saucepan placed over medium heat.
2. Peel the plantains under running water. Slice them into ½-inch rounds, and soak them in warm, salted water to cover for 10 minutes.
3. Drain the slices, and place them on paper towels. Make sure the slices are thoroughly dry.
4. Deep-fry the plantain in safflower oil in a deep-frier or small, high-sided pan. The oil should reach 350°F. A wok works well for deep-frying and takes less oil.
5. When the slices turn from pink to a golden color, remove and drain them on paper towels.
6. Place 2 cups of the broth with the plantains in a blender or food processor, and blend until creamy. Add the salt and the remaining broth, and blend.
7. Heat the soup, and serve it with a spoonful of cheese garnish on each serving.

Serves 4

Golden Saffron Buns

1 T yeast
½ C warm milk
2 t saffron threads
½ C water
2 T sweet butter
1 T honey
1 t salt
1 extra large egg, slightly beaten
  grated rind of 1 lemon
¼ t allspice
¼ C golden raisins
1 T pine nuts
2½ to 3 C unbleached all-purpose flour

1. Dissolve the yeast in the milk.
2. Bring the saffron threads and water to a boil, cover, remove from the heat, and steep for 5 minutes.
3. Melt the butter with the honey. Combine the butter and saffron mixtures with the yeast mixture when the liquids are cool so as not to kill the yeast.
4. Add the salt, egg, lemon rind, allspice, raisins, and nuts.
5. Stir in the flour. Place on a flat surface, and knead for 5 minutes, adding flour to prevent sticking.
6. Place dough in an oiled bowl, turn over so the top is coated with oil, cover with a cloth, and let rise in a warm spot until nearly doubled in bulk (about 1½ hours).
7. Punch down dough, and form into a cylinder. Mark 12 equal sections. Cut the sections, and form buns by tucking the dough into its center until the top is round and smooth. Place in a large, oiled baking pan. Cover and let rise until doubled in bulk (about 1 hour).
8. Bake at 375°F for 15 to 20 minutes or until done.

Yields 12 buns

Deviled Eggs

4 hard-boiled extra large eggs, peeled
2 T mayonnaise
1/4 t prepared Dijon-style mustard
1/4 t wine vinegar
1/4 t Tabasco sauce
1/4 t Worcestershire sauce
    dash of paprika
    lettuce greens

1. Cut each egg in half lengthwise, keeping the halves paired. Remove the yolks, and place them in a dish. Reserve the whites.
2. To the yolks, add the mayonnaise, mustard, vinegar, sauces, and paprika. Mash with a fork until the yolks are creamy. Add more mayonnaise if the yolks are too dry.
3. With a knife, spread the yolks back into the whites. Sprinkle with paprika, and serve them on a bed of lettuce.

Serves 4

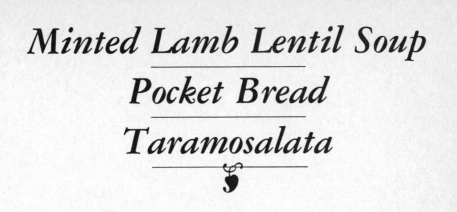

Minted Lamb Lentil Soup

Pocket Bread

Taramosalata

The Soup. Lamb and mint appear as companions in many recipes, complementing each other with their strong, pervasive flavors. This soup is of Greek origin. To heighten the spectrum of colors, you can use both red and green sweet peppers and red and green lentils.

The Bread. You may know these pocket breads by many names—peda, pita, Syrian bread, Armenian flatbread, Greek bread, Middle Eastern bread. They all have pockets, and, cut in half, they're handy "half moon" breads that you can fill with endless sandwich possibilities, including the Greek lamb souvlakia, Middle Eastern chick pea felafel, and American chives-and-scrambled egg on mayo. Also, you can cut one side of the halves into wedges; butter them; season with your choice of herbs, spices, cheese, or garlic; and crisp them under the broiler. The Lebanese Zahtar (see p. 201) is an example of fitting pocket bread to a particular meal.

The Salad. This classic Greek dish has a traditional variation—blending in some cream cheese while reducing the oil. Always serve this dish with hot bread.

Drink suggestion: Greek retsina wine

Minted Lamb Lentil Soup

   5 C water
   1 C beef broth
1½ C red or green lentils
   1 t salt
   4 T virgin olive oil
   1 C peeled and diced yellow onion
   1 large clove garlic, peeled, crushed, and minced
¾ C seeded, cored, and diced sweet red pepper
   1 C scraped and diced carrots
   2 T dried peppermint (or fresh, if available)
½ t basil
½ t marjoram
⅛ t thyme
      black pepper, freshly ground
½ lb lean ground lamb
   2 C peeled tomatoes, with juice
½ C water
   2 T fresh lemon juice

1. Pour the water and broth into a large soup kettle. Add the lentils and salt, and bring them to a boil. Lower the heat to medium, and continue to cook the lentils at a slow boil for 30 minutes.
2. Heat the olive oil in a large skillet over high heat.
3. Add the onions, garlic, sweet pepper, carrots, and herbs to the oil. Pass the pepper mill over the simmering vegetables. Cover the skillet, and cook the vegetables over medium heat for 10 minutes.
4. Add the lamb, stirring it into the simmering vegetables. Leave the mixture uncovered, and continue simmering for 5 minutes. (If lamb is fatty, drain off excess oil.)
5. Add tomatoes and juice to the lentils along with the sautéed

vegetables and the lamb, cleaning out the skillet with ½ cup of water and adding this to the soup kettle.

6. Cook the soup, covered, over medium heat for 40 minutes until all of the flavors are blended. Stir in the lemon juice just before serving.

Serves 6

Pocket Bread

2 *T yeast*
½ *C warm water*
1½ *C water*
1 *T salt*
pinch of sugar
2 *T oil*
5 to 6 *C unbleached all-purpose flour*
cornmeal

1. Dissolve the yeast in the warm water.
2. Add the 1½ cups water, salt, sugar, and oil.
3. Stir in 3 cups of flour before adding 2 more cups. Place dough on a flat surface, and knead 8 to 10 minutes, adding flour to prevent sticking.
4. Place dough in an oiled bowl, turn over so the top is coated with oil, cover with a cloth, and let rise in a warm spot until doubled in bulk (about 1½ hours).
5. Punch down dough, and on a flat surface form the dough into a cylinder. Cut into 10 equal parts. For each part, make a smooth ball; then flatten it with the palms of your hands. On a floured flat surface, roll it into a 5-inch round between ¼ inch and ⅛ inch thick. Place dough on an oiled baking sheet sprinkled with cornmeal.

6. Bake at 500°F for 6 to 7 minutes, turning the heat to 400°F immediately after you put the breads in the oven. The breads will puff up so that the insides are hollow. Place them in a plastic bag to cool; their outsides will remain soft due to the retained moisture.

Yields 10 pocket breads

Taramosalata

¼ lb smoked cod roe
½ C fresh white bread crumbs
1 clove garlic, peeled and pressed
2 T heavy cream
  juice of 1 lemon
½ C olive oil
  salt and pepper to taste
  paprika

1. Mix the roe, bread crumbs, and garlic in a bowl. Beat in the cream.
2. Beat in the lemon juice and oil until the mixture is smooth.
3. Add the salt and pepper. Place artfully in a serving dish, and sprinkle with paprika. Serve at room temperature.

Serves 4

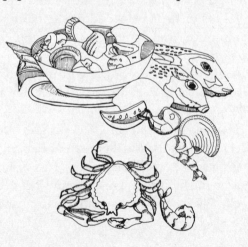

Red Pepper Soup (Cold)
Soda Bread
Wild Rice Salad

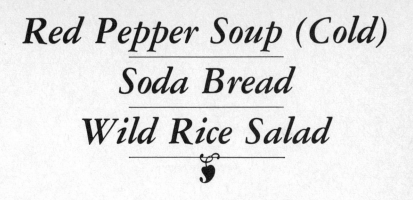

The Soup. Red peppers are sweet green globe peppers ripened until they are red. Be sure to buy sweet peppers, not hot chile peppers. This is a very healthy soup. One red pepper contains more of vitamins A and C than an orange. The soup has, as they say in the vernacular, everything going for it—a zingy color, a delicious and unusual flavor, and body-building nutrition.

The Bread. Here's one of the quickest breads you can bake—perfect for hot summer days. This version is a basic soda bread. You can vary it by adding melted sweet butter, sugar, and currants; however, it then becomes more of a sweet bread than a traditional Irish farm loaf with thrifty, handy ingredients. At breakfast, try this as buttermilk toast spread with sweet butter and apricot jam.

The Salad. Native to North America, wild rice is the seed of a freshwater and swamp grass that grows 12 feet high in the Southeast, 4 feet in the North. You can find it in relative abundance in Wisconsin, Minnesota, and Michigan, where it is harvested mostly in the wild and shipped to fine markets nationally. The nutty flavor and crunchy texture scarcely resemble white or brown rice, although you can use it in similar dishes—and with twice the pleasure.

Drink suggestion: extra-dry champagne

Red Pepper Soup (Cold)

6 T *sweet butter*
2 C *well-washed and sliced leeks (white part only)*
3 C *cored, seeded, and diced sweet red peppers (approximately 1 lb of whole peppers)*
2½ C *chicken broth*
  salt and white pepper to taste
2 C *buttermilk*

1. Melt the butter in a large saucepan, and add the leeks. (One bunch of four medium-size leeks equals approximately 2 cups.) Cover the leeks, and sweat them over low heat for 5 minutes.
2. Add the sweet red peppers, cover, and continue to sweat the vegetables 20 minutes or until they're limp. Place a piece of waxed paper under the lid to create a better seal.
3. Add the chicken broth and simmer the soup, covered, for 30 minutes.
4. Add salt and pepper to taste.
5. Cool, and blend the ingredients in batches in a blender or food processor.
6. Add the buttermilk only when the soup reaches room temperature.
7. Place the soup in a covered container, and refrigerate it for 4 hours or until it is well chilled.

Serves 4

Soda Bread

   2   C unbleached all-purpose flour
1½   t baking powder
  ½   t baking soda
  ½   t salt
   1   extra large egg, well beaten
  ⅞   C buttermilk

1. Mix the flour, baking powder, baking soda, and salt.
2. Pour two-thirds of the egg into the flour mixture. Add the buttermilk in thirds, beating it into the flour mixture until a thick dough forms.
3. Place dough on a flat surface and knead 2 or 3 minutes until the dough becomes smooth and elastic, adding flour to prevent sticking.
4. Place the dough in an oiled, round, 1-quart baking dish; then flatten dough with your hand. With a sharp knife, cut a cross about ¼ inch deep over the entire top. Brush the entire top with the rest of the beaten egg.
5. Bake at 375°F for 30 minutes or until done. Serve warm or cold.

Yields 1 loaf

Wild Rice Salad

  ⅔   C uncooked wild rice
       salted water to cover
   1   chicken breast, filleted
   1   T sweet butter
   1   T olive oil
  ¼   C sliced water chestnuts

DRESSING
4 T walnut oil
2 t balsamic vinegar
salt and pepper to taste

romaine lettuce

1. Prepare the wild rice by covering it with 3 inches of salted water and boiling uncovered for 30 minutes or until tender. Drain and then steam it for 15 to 20 minutes until the grains split open. Cool.
2. Sauté the chicken lightly in butter and oil, cooking gently and thoroughly; do not overcook the chicken. Cool and shred the chicken into bite-size pieces.
3. Place the wild rice in a bowl, and mix in the chicken and water chestnuts.
4. For the dressing, mix the oil, vinegar, salt, and pepper. Pour over the wild rice mixture.
5. Place two to three romaine leaves on each plate, and spoon the wild rice mixture onto the leaves.

Serves 4

Shark's Fin Soup
Fried Scallion Cakes
Chinese Cabbage Salad

The Soup. We first tasted this soup at an excellent Chinese restaurant in Brooklyn. It takes a great deal of preparation time. We suggest a celebration for serving this soup because of the expense and time involved.

Lay out the ingredients and bowls for the various steps ahead of time. Look for shark's fin in the Chinese section of most larger cities. The cake also goes by the name of "needles" and looks somewhat like a mass of dried rawhide. The abiding instruction of my Chinese grocer was, "Boil. Boil." When cooked, it looks very much like slightly cooked egg. Though the odor at first is fishy, the fin transforms into a delicately flavored essence blended into an exquisitely balanced soup.

The Bread. Be sure to start kneading the warm dough as soon as you pour in the boiling water, which softens the stretchable gluten. You can use these pancakes for Peking duck, mo-shu pork, and other dishes. For other addictive tidbits, substitute chives, parsley, or onions. The process may appear long, but once you get the rhythm, you'll finish in a half hour.

The Salad. Bok choy is also known as Chinese cabbage, sin choy as Chinese celery cabbage. Together they make a sweet, juicy, simple combination. Sesame seed oil is vigorously aromatic. A little goes a long way (used for flavoring not for cooking because it has a low smoking point and overpowering taste).

Drink suggestion: jasmine tea

Shark's Fin Soup

1 (7-oz) shark's fin cake (sometimes called "needles")
   cold water
2 scallions
2 slices ginger, peeled
¼ lb thinly sliced uncooked loin pork (from 1 loin chop)
2 t dark soy sauce
1 t rice wine
½ t Oriental sesame seed oil
1 slice gingerroot, peeled and crushed with side of cleaver
   or pricked with a fork
1 T rice wine
1 egg white, whipped until foamy
1 t cornstarch
¼ lb thinly sliced, uncooked, boned chicken breast (from
   split chicken breast)
6 C chicken broth
4 T rice wine
2 T cornstarch
1 t sugar
2 T rice wine vinegar
2 t Worcestershire sauce
1 t peeled and minced gingerroot
1 t Oriental sesame seed oil
2 T thinly sliced scallions (bottom 3 inches)
¼ t Chinese hot chile sauce (or Tabasco sauce)
¼ lb thinly sliced cooked ham (½-inch strips)

1. Place the shark's fin cake (needles) in a large kettle. Add cold water to cover it. Add one scallion and a piece of ginger. Bring the fin to a boil over high heat. Cover the kettle. Reduce the heat, and simmer the fin for 45 minutes. Drain and rinse the shark's fin. Return it to the kettle, and repeat the above process.

2. In a bowl, marinate the pork strips in 2 teaspoons of soy sauce, 1 teaspoon of rice wine, and ½ teaspoon Oriental sesame seed oil.

3. In another bowl, soak the gingerroot in 1 tablespoon of rice wine so that the flavor infuses into the gingerroot for 5 minutes.
4. Remove the gingerroot and stir the egg white, cornstarch, and chicken into the rice wine. Set this mixture aside.
5. Heat the chicken broth over medium heat.
6. In a cup, combine the 4 tablespoons of rice wine with 2 tablespoons of cornstarch, sugar, and rice wine vinegar.
7. In a separate bowl, mix 2 teaspoons of Worcestershire sauce, 1 teaspoon of minced gingerroot, 1 teaspoon Oriental sesame seed oil, 2 tablespoons of scallions, and ¼ teaspoon of hot chile sauce.
8. Remove the ginger and scallions from the well-drained and rinsed shark's fin. Add the fin to the heated chicken broth.
9. Add the pork mixture, chicken mixture, scallion seasoning mixture, and sliced, cooked ham to the soup kettle.
10. When the soup is just bubbling, stir the cornstarch once in the cup, and add it to the soup. Slowly boil the soup for 2 to 3 minutes until the broth thickens and clears.

Serves 6

Fried Scallion Cakes

1 C unbleached all-purpose flour
¼ C plus 2 T boiling water
sesame seed oil

FILLING
1 medium egg, beaten
salt
⅓ C chopped scallions (about 4 to 5 scallions)

peanut oil

1. For the pancakes, place the flour in a mixing bowl, form a depression in the center, and pour the water into it. Beat vigorously until the dough forms a ball.
2. Knead dough on a flat surface for 8 to 10 minutes until it is smooth and elastic. Cover dough with a cloth, and let rest for 10 minutes.
3. Meanwhile, prepare the egg and scallions for the filling.
4. To make the pancakes, roll the dough into a circle ¼ inch thick. With a 2-inch biscuit cutter or glass top, cut out eight rounds.
5. Coat the top of one round completely and generously with sesame seed oil. Place a second round on top. Roll both together into a 6-inch circle (the pancakes will be very thin).
6. Cook the pancakes 2 to 3 minutes on an ungreased iron skillet over medium heat until they are spotted light brown on the bottom. Turn them over, and cook the other side (the pancakes will bubble irregularly between the two sides).
7. Remove the pancakes from the skillet, and gently peel the halves apart; the sesame seed oil helps keep them separate. Place them in a plastic bag to retain their pliability.
8. To fill each pancake, lay the cooked side down, brush the face-up side with egg, and sprinkle lightly with salt. Scatter on some scallions, and loosely roll up the pancakes.
9. Fry the cakes in hot peanut oil until brown and crisp on all sides (about 1 minute). Remove to an absorbent paper towel. On a cutting board, slice each cake three times on the diagonal, and serve.

Serves 4

Chinese Cabbage Salad

2 C loosely packed sliced bok choy
2 C loosely packed sliced sin choy
  shredded carrots

DRESSING
2 T white rice vinegar
2 t sesame seed oil
  salt to taste

1. Separate the branches of the bok choy, and slice the white base only into ¼-inch-wide pieces.
2. Separate the branches of the sin choy, and slice the top sections with the green into ¼-inch-wide pieces. Mix the two cabbages, and place on serving plates.
3. With a vegetable peeler or paring knife, scrape the long edges of a cut carrot over the cabbages to make very thin julienne strips. Add only 8 to 10 carrot strips to each salad.
4. For the dressing, blend the vinegar and oil; then pour over the salads. Sprinkle the salad lightly with salt. Chill and serve.

Serves 4

Black Bean Soup
Bacon Spoon Bread
Avocado with Mexican Salsa

The Soup. Black Bean Soup is striking served in everyday white bowls. Mexican pottery and bright napkins also offset the black, a color that rarely appears in nature. The chile content is at the cook's discretion. As they say of Mexican food, you eat with your right hand and wipe your nose with the left.

The Bread. Serve and eat Bacon Spoon Bread with a spoon, as its name implies. This particular version is smooth and light. Be sure to serve it hot straight from the oven and with slabs of butter seeping down the individual portions. It's important not to overbake the bread. You can cook into the bread an intriguing, edgy taste by substituting buttermilk for the sweet milk.

The Salad. If you like a sauce that's on the edge of ignition, green salsa fits the bill; however, you can adjust this version for its flammability as you prepare it. If you like it hot, keep all the pepper seeds; if not, discard some of them. It's imperative to use rubber gloves when handling the jalapeño so that later you won't touch your fingers absentmindedly to your eyes and lips, stinging and burning them. Cilantro is like a sparse, flat-leafed parsley and, in fact, is known as Chinese parsley. Cilantro is coriander, and the seeds of the plant appear much in other cooking, especially baking.

Drink suggestion: Mexican beer

Black Bean Soup

1 C dried black beans
   water to cover
⅛ lb salt pork (blanch with boiling water)
2 C chicken broth
1 ripe tomato, diced
4 C cold water
2 cloves garlic, peeled, crushed, and minced
½ C peeled and diced onion
¼ t hot jalapeño pepper sauce
½ t imported oregano
1½ T virgin olive oil
1 t salt
   black pepper, freshly ground
2 T dry sherry
   sour cream

1. Wash the beans, place them in a kettle, and cover them with water. Bring them to a boil over high heat. Cover and remove them from the burner. Leave them covered for 2 to 3 hours.
2. Place the drained beans, salt pork, chicken broth, tomato, and cold water in a large soup kettle. Bring them to a boil. Reduce the heat, and cover the kettle. Cook the beans at a slow boil for 1½ to 2 hours.
3. Sauté the garlic, onion, chile pepper sauce, and oregano in olive oil until the onion is golden. Add this mixture to the beans.
4. Add salt and pepper.
5. Reserve 1 cup of the beans. Place the remainder in a food processor or blender, and purée them for a few minutes until smooth.
6. Reheat all of the ingredients (including the reserved beans) for 5 minutes. Stir in the sherry.
7. Ladle the soup into bowls, and float a dollop of sour cream in each.

Serves 4

Bacon Spoon Bread

4 rashers lean bacon
2 C milk
½ t salt
1 C white cornmeal
2 extra large eggs, separated
¾ t sugar
  pinch of white pepper
3 T sweet butter

1. Broil the bacon, and reserve the fat. Brush a 1-quart baking dish with the bacon grease. After the bacon is cool and crisp, break it into small pieces; set aside.
2. In a heavy saucepan, heat the milk and salt to the simmer point.
3. Slowly pour in the cornmeal while stirring the milk mixture. Continue stirring until the mixture becomes very thick. Remove from the heat to cool slightly.
4. Beat in the egg yolks, the remainder of the bacon fat, bacon pieces, sugar, pepper, and butter.
5. Beat the egg whites at room temperature until stiff. Fold the whites into the cornmeal mixture. Pour into the prepared baking dish, and smooth the top.
6. Bake at 350°F for 20 to 30 minutes. The center of the spoon bread should be moist and light, slightly undercooked. Serve warm with sweet butter.

Serves 4

Avocado with Mexican Salsa

2 ripe avocados
lettuce greens

DRESSING
1 green jalapeño pepper, diced
1 T finely chopped fresh cilantro leaves
4 scallions, finely chopped (including the stem until it separates)
½ t dry mustard
¼ t salt
pinch of cayenne
⅓ C skinned and chopped tomatoes
1 T corn oil
1 t red wine vinegar
tomato juice to thin

1. Peel the avocados, cut in half lengthwise, and remove the seed. Slice the halves vertically in ½-inch strips, and lay the avocado on a bed of lettuce.
2. For the dressing, cut off and discard the stem of the pepper before dicing it.
3. Add the cilantro, scallions, mustard, salt, cayenne, tomatoes, oil, and vinegar. Mix well. If needed, add the tomato juice to thin the sauce. Serve alongside the avocado.

Serves 4

Scungilli Soup
Chewy Rolls
Endive and Escarole Salad

The Soup. Floridians eat the conch, or giant sea whelk, in a Southern-style chowder using evaporated milk and ground conch. Scungilli is the Italian name for this deep ocean dweller.

Anyone disliking the chewy texture of abalone will not care for scungilli. It is a "tough customer," requiring pounding with a meat hammer and marinating. Mincing the meat also breaks down its muscular texture. Leaving it to slowly steam on its own for a few hours tames this ornery univalve, too.

Look for scungilli in an Italian or Chinese market. The conical shell of the whelk spans 5 to 7 inches, forming a whorled beauty. The creature inside, however, presents less than a princely aspect to the unsuspecting cook. All around, scungilli will be a new experience leading to a taste of the deep, deep sea.

The Bread. With a thick, dark crust, these are fist-and-teeth-ripping rolls. Great with this soup, they don't keep long; so it's best to use them soon after baking. The egg whites, the steam-bath, and no oil give them their chewy texture.

The Salad. The sweetish side of this dressing balances the piquancy of the greens, known and enjoyed for their striking taste. You can substitute dandelion greens for the escarole, or, for that matter, add them for another dimension.

Drink suggestion: Valpolicella wine

Scungilli Soup

1 1/4 lb fresh or frozen conch meat
1/2 C lime juice
1/2 C cold water
4 C chicken broth
2 C peeled whole Italian plum tomatoes, with juice
2 T pesto (minced basil and parsley in virgin olive oil)
1/4 t imported oregano
3/4 C dry white wine
    water
1/2 C spaghettini (thin spaghetti), broken into 1-inch pieces
    salt to taste

1. Cut the white-to-gray meat from the shucked conch into large pieces. Discard the foot of the conch, the valve, and the black sac. A pound and a quarter will yield about 2 cups of meat. Pound the conch well with a meat hammer for 2 to 3 minutes or until the meat is flexible and pulpy. Mince the conch meat with a mezza luna or a sharp knife. The smaller the mince, the more tender the scungilli.

2. Let the minced conch marinate in lime juice and water in a covered casserole for 1 hour. Drain and rinse it.

3. Place the chicken broth and plum tomatoes together in a soup kettle.

4. Heat the pesto over low heat in a medium-size stainless steel skillet. Add oregano, and gently simmer the herbs a few minutes.

5. Add the scungilli and white wine. Turn up the heat slightly, and simmer the scungilli for 15 minutes.

6. Boil the chicken broth and tomatoes. Reduce the heat, and add the scungilli and wine. Cover the soup, and cook it for 1 hour. Keep the kettle covered, setting the soup aside at room temperature for a few hours. It will continue to cook in its own steam.

7. Fifteen minutes before serving the Scungilli Soup, boil water in a large kettle. Add the spaghettini, and boil the pasta for 10 minutes or until it is al dente (firm to the bite).
8. Drain the pasta, and add it to the soup. Correct the soup for salt. Italians usually don't eat Parmesan cheese with shellfish, but it's your choice.

Serves 4

Chewy Rolls

2 T yeast
½ C warm water
1 C water
1 T (scant) salt
1 t sugar
2 egg whites
4 C unbleached all-purpose flour
cornmeal

GLAZE
1 egg yolk
1 T water

1. Dissolve the yeast in the warm water.
2. Stir in the rest of the water, salt, sugar, and egg whites. Beat in 3 cups flour. On a flat surface, knead dough 8 to 10 minutes, adding flour to prevent sticking.
3. Place dough in an oiled bowl, turn over so the top is coated with oil, cover with a cloth, and let rise in a warm spot until doubled in bulk (about 1½ hours).
4. Punch down dough, and on a flat surface form into a cylinder.

Cut into 16 equal parts. Shape each part into smooth, dome-shaped rolls. Place on oiled baking sheets sprinkled with cornmeal. Cover and let rise until fully doubled in bulk (about 1 hour).

5. For the glaze, beat the egg yolk and water together. Brush the rolls with the egg wash.

6. Place a large, flat pan of boiling water on a low rack in the oven; then bake the rolls at 400°F for 15 to 20 minutes or until done.

Yields 16 rolls

Endive and Escarole Salad

shredded endive and escarole for 4

DRESSING
4 *T olive oil*
1 *T cider vinegar*
1 *T sugar*
1 *T minced scallion*
½ *t salt*
½ *t dry mustard*
1 *t poppy seeds*

1. Prepare the lettuces, and place them in a large serving bowl.

2. For the dressing, mix the oil, vinegar, sugar, scallions, salt, mustard, and poppy seeds. Whisk thoroughly to dissolve the sugar. Immediately before serving, pour over the salad.

Serves 4

Oxtail Consommé Julienne
Scottish Oatcakes
Chicken Cranberry Salad

The Soup.   Clarification is a magical process that turns cloudy broth into a clear liquid. You can see straight to the bottom of the cup, like a glass-bottomed boat in limpid tropical waters. Glass bowls or cups enhance the scintillating shimmer of the consommé.

The Bread.   These are quick and handy, made with all-American ingredients found in nearly any household. You can substitute quick rolled oats, but we find that standard rolled oats give a better texture and firmer taste. These are so simple that their goodness defies detection on sight alone. Try them once and be convinced.

The Salad.   Originally named by New England pilgrims as the craneberry (its stamen resembling the bill of a crane), cranberries are nearly always sweetened to balance their tartness, adding zest to any dish. Cultivated bogs on Cape Cod in Massachusetts produce a major portion of cranberries that are turned into everything from fruit juice to pies. This salad is a good opportunity to use leftover chicken from stock that you made for soups.

Drink suggestion: cold milk

Oxtail Consommé Julienne

> 1½ to 2 lb oxtail (cut into 1-inch pieces)
> 2 small onions, peeled and quartered
> 2 T corn oil
> 8 C cold water
>
> BOUQUET GARNI
> ½ bay leaf
> 3 sprigs celery
> 3 sprigs parsley
> 6 peppercorns, crushed
> cheesecloth
> kitchen thread
>
> cheesecloth
> 1 t salt
> 2 egg whites and shells
> 2 t red currant jelly
> 2 T sherry
> ½ C julienne strips (matchstick-thin) carrot
> ½ C julienne strips celery

1. Over high heat in a heavy soup kettle (and with the kitchen window open or fan on), brown the oxtail and onions in hot oil. Char the oxtail pieces and onions to make a darker consommé.
2. Add the water, and boil the oxtail. Tie the bouquet garni into a square of cheesecloth, and drop it into the broth.
3. Cook the soup, covered, simmering it for 1½ hours.
4. Place cheesecloth in a large strainer over a bowl. Strain the stock into the bowl, reserving the oxtails for another meal. Discard the bouquet garni. Add the salt.
5. Refrigerate the oxtail broth overnight or until the fat has congealed on top.
6. To clarify, carefully remove all fat with a slotted spoon; then pour the consommé through another round of double cheesecloth

to extract every fat globule. Add the egg whites and crushed shells to the *cold* consommé, and pour it into a clean stainless-steel pan. Whisk the consommé to distribute the egg whites and shells while the consommé heats to a boil. Just after the egg white foams to the top, reduce the heat so the consommé remains at a steady simmer, boiling just below the surface. Stop whisking, and let the egg do its trick. It will bob to the top, carrying the impurities with it. Simmer the consommé for 20 minutes. Carefully ladle the consommé from under the egg froth and into double cheesecloth placed in a clean strainer over a deep bowl.

7. Add the currant jelly, sherry, and julienne vegetables to the consommé in the bowl and return it to a clean stainless steel pan, boiling it for another 5 minutes. Again, egg froth might appear on the top, so merely skim this off the surface with a slotted spoon. A sparkling clear consommé will appear underneath.

Serves 4

Scottish Oatcakes

1 C *unbleached all-purpose flour*
1 T *sugar*
1 t *baking powder*
½ t *salt*
2 C *rolled oats*
½ C *sweet butter*
½ C *milk*

1. Combine the flour, sugar, baking powder, and salt.
2. Stir in the oats. With a pastry blender or two knives, cut in the butter.

3. Gradually stir in the milk until the dough forms a ball.
4. On a lightly floured flat surface, roll the dough into a rectangle to ⅛-inch thickness. You may need to keep the rolling pin floured to prevent sticking.
5. Cut in half to manageable size, and place on a greased baking sheet.
6. Bake at 375°F for 12 to 15 minutes or until slightly browned.
7. Remove from the oven; with a sharp knife, cut individual servings to the size of two parallel fingers. Serve warm.

Serves 6

Chicken Cranberry Salad

¼ C sour cream
2 oz softened cream cheese
1 C diced cooked chicken
½ C diced celery
½ C chopped walnuts
　 salt and white pepper to taste
　 Bibb lettuce leaves
　 jellied cranberry sauce
　 parsley sprigs

1. Blend the sour cream and softened cream cheese until smooth.
2. Mix in the chicken, celery, and walnuts. Add the salt and pepper.
3. On the lettuce, place a ¼-inch-thick circle of cranberry sauce. Place a scoop of chicken mixture on the cranberry. Garnish with a sprig of parsley. Chill and serve.

Serves 4

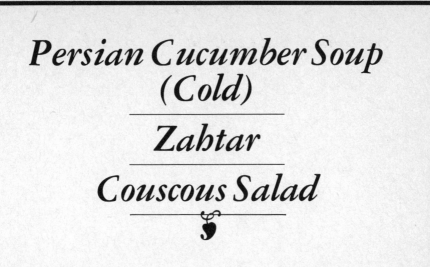

Persian Cucumber Soup (Cold)

Zahtar

Couscous Salad

The Soup. This soup is effortless to make on those hot, humid summer days when it seems difficult to lift a finger. It's a refreshing, white, mystical poem.

The Bread. Red powdered sumac has an intriguing, off-center, lemony taste; in fact, you can make it into a "lemonade" drink. Look for sumac in most natural foods stores. You can vary this basic Lebanese zahtar of sumac and thyme by adding toasted sesame seeds, finely chopped pistachio nuts, or oregano.

The Salad. Couscous is coarsely ground semolina or wheat grain that steams into a wonderfully light texture. A Middle Eastern stew with the grain mixed into the broth is also called couscous. If you don't have a steamer or couscousier, put the grain in a strainer, cover, and place over a pot of slowly boiling water. As a salad, couscous is a refreshing change of pace.

Drink suggestion: orzata (almond syrup) in soda water

Persian Cucumber Soup (Cold)

2 T golden raisins
1 C hot water
1 C peeled, seeded, diced, and tightly packed cucumber
1 T virgin olive oil
1 t wine vinegar
1 t salt
2 T finely sliced scallions (bottom 3 inches only)
    black pepper, freshly ground
2 C plain yogurt
½ C ice water
1 C heavy cream
3 T chopped walnut meats
1 T destemmed and minced fresh dill (dried dill may be substituted)

1. Soak the raisins in boiling hot water for 1 hour to plump them. Drain them, and set aside.
2. Prepare the cucumber. Place it in a bowl and mix in the olive oil, wine vinegar, salt, and scallions. Make three or four turns with the pepper mill over the bowl.
3. Place the yogurt, ice water, and heavy cream in a mixing bowl. Stir in the walnut meats, dill, and cucumber mixture.
4. Add the softened raisins. Chill the soup until ready to serve. (The raisins tend to sink, so use a ladle to bring them up from the bottom.)

Serves 4

Zahtar

2 small Pocket Breads (see p. 175 for recipe)
1 T sumac powder
1 T thyme
olive oil

1. Cut the pocket breads in half. By hand, separate the halves so that you have four "half moons" of the breads. Cut three equal wedges from each half.
2. In a small bowl, mix the sumac and thyme together.
3. Generously brush olive oil onto the wedges.
4. Sprinkle on the sumac mixture.
5. Transfer the wedges to a baking sheet, and place under the broiler until lightly crisped.

Yields 12 bread triangles

Couscous Salad

¾ C couscous
1 C water
¼ C pine nuts
2 scallions, bottom 3
   inches, chopped
½ C destemmed chopped
   parsley

DRESSING
3 T walnut oil
2 t wine vinegar
salt and pepper to taste

Bibb lettuce leaves

1. Soak the couscous in the water until it is absorbed (about 20 minutes).
2. Place the couscous in a steamer, and steam for 30 minutes.
3. Meanwhile, lightly toast the pine nuts by stirring them constantly in an iron skillet over medium heat.
4. Prepare the scallions and parsley.
5. Separate the couscous grains by working them gently with a fork or your fingers so that they're light and fluffy. Stir in the pine nuts, scallions, and parsley.
6. For the dressing, blend the oil, vinegar, salt, and pepper. Pour over the salad, mix, and serve on the lettuce.

Serves 4

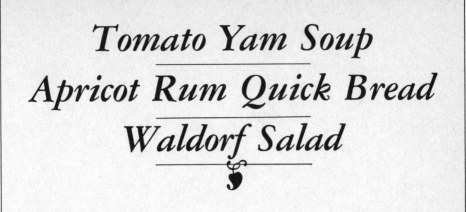

Tomato Yam Soup
Apricot Rum Quick Bread
Waldorf Salad

The Soup. This soup produces a psychedelic color and a sweet, earthy taste. Yams are similar to sweet potatoes but have a higher moisture and sugar content.

The Bread. A rich golden-amber, this not-too-sweet bread has a soft interior under a mahogany crust. The apricot purée combined with the apricot pieces gives a double taste treat. Another gentle way to rehydrate the dried fruit is to cover them with plenty of water, and let them soak overnight. A food processor purées them in a few seconds.

The Salad. The maître d' of the Waldorf-Astoria Hotel in New York City supposedly invented this salad, originally of only tiny apple and celery pieces (the walnuts were added anonymously and permanently later). Use Cortland or a similar sweet apple that retains the white inside a long time before discoloring from oxygen exposure, although the mayonnaise helps to retard the discoloration. Find a quality sugarless prepared mayonnaise, or make your own, to finish off this simple, appealing salad.

Drink suggestion: cold milk

Tomato Yam Soup

3 small leeks, washed well and thinly sliced (white part only)
2 T sweet butter
2 soft ripe tomatoes, peeled and seeded
2½ C chicken broth
½ t salt
½ t destemmed and minced fresh basil
1 C cooked (baked or boiled) fresh yams
salt to taste

1. Sauté the sliced leeks in butter, cover the pan, and simmer the leeks over low heat for 5 minutes.
2. Slice the tomatoes, and add them to the leeks.
3. Add 1 cup of the chicken broth, salt, and basil. Cover and simmer the soup for 10 minutes.
4. Place the broth, tomatoes, and leeks in a blender or food processor, and purée them for 2 to 3 minutes.
5. Return this mixture to a saucepan.
6. Blend the cooked yams with the remaining 1½ cups of chicken broth.
7. Add the yam mixture to the saucepan, and bring the soup to a boil.
8. Add salt if necessary.

Serves 4

Apricot Rum Quick Bread

1 C dried apricots
water to cover
1¾ C unbleached all-purpose flour
1 t baking soda
½ t salt
¼ C sweet butter
½ C sugar
1 extra large egg, slightly beaten
2 T dark rum
¾ C buttermilk
⅓ C apricot jam for glaze

1. Rehydrate the apricots by submerging them in 3 inches of water in a large saucepan, cover, and bring to a boil. Turn off the heat, and leave the pan on the burner. The apricots will reconstitute gently in less than 1 hour. Reserve ½ cup apricot halves, and purée the rest.
2. Mix the flour, soda, and salt in a small bowl.
3. Cream the butter and sugar in a medium-size bowl. Beat in the egg. Add the rum and ¾ cup apricot purée.
4. Alternate beating the buttermilk and flour mixture into the butter mixture.
5. Cut the remaining rehydrated apricots into bite-size pieces, and fold them into the batter.
6. Pour the batter into an oiled 8½ x 4½ x 2½-inch loaf dish. Bake at 375°F for 50 to 60 minutes or until a knife inserted in the center comes out clean.
7. For the glaze, heat and strain the jam. Brush onto the top of the loaf.

Yields 1 loaf

Waldorf Salad

1 C chopped, threaded celery, without leaves
1 C chopped cored apple
½ C chopped walnuts
3 T mayonnaise
4 Boston lettuce leaves

1. Chop the celery, apples, and walnuts approximately the same size, in ½-inch chunks.
2. Stir in the mayonnaise to coat the ingredients. Chill.
3. Serve on individual beds of lettuce leaves.

Serves 4

Pane e Pomodoro Soup

Country Italian

Radicchio Salad

The Soup. Bread soup has been a staple diet the world over. Europeans pour hot water over bread and simply season with a little salt and pepper. Here in Amerca we are more familiar with milk toast as a panacea for the invalid with a "poor" stomach. This bread and tomato soup adds some pizzazz to bread soup with a blend of Mediterranean tastes. Pane e Pomodoro (bread with tomato) tastes best at the height of tomato season with vine-ripe tomatoes and freshly picked basil.

The Bread. This sturdy loaf works well for the accompanying Pane e Pomodoro. The crust is hard and the interior firm, a good headstart in preparing the soup. Leftover Country Italian also makes good French toast. Soak slices of the *pain perdu* in eggs, fry in sweet butter, and douse them with true maple syrup—Country Italian becoming farmhouse French becoming Sunday morning American.

The Salad. Radicchio is a small, red-purplish head of lettuce favored in Italy. Apply the dressing at serving time because the fragile Boston lettuce will wilt. This has an international cast to it—Boston, Rome, and Tokyo. Umeboshi is a red plum vinegar with salt. It's a by-product of the process of making pickled ume, or Japanese plums. If you offer wine with this soup combination, serve it before the salad, because the wine and dressing will conflict.

Drink suggestion: Soave Italian wine

Pane e Pomodoro Soup

3 C chicken broth
4 C water
¼ C virgin olive oil
2 large cloves garlic, peeled, crushed, and minced
1 t minced fresh basil leaves
½ lb sliced Italian bread (see p. 209) (exposed to air for
a few days)
2 C peeled, cored, and chopped fresh tomatoes, with juice
salt to taste
black pepper, freshly ground

1. Bring the chicken broth and water to a boil in a large soup
   kettle.
2. Heat the olive oil in a large skillet.
3. Sauté the garlic and basil in the oil over medium heat. When
   the garlic turns golden, add the bread slices.
4. Press down on each slice of bread with a spatula to flavor and
   brown it lightly on each side. Remove the bread from the skillet.
5. Add tomatoes to the skillet, and boil them over high heat for
   3 minutes. Add them to the hot chicken broth, cover the kettle,
   and simmer the broth and tomatoes over low heat for 30 minutes.
   Taste and correct the soup for salt.
6. Sprinkle the soup liberally with freshly ground black pepper.
7. Place the bread slices in flat soup plates, and pour the tomato
   soup over the bread.

Serves 4

Country Italian

1 T yeast
½ C warm water
  pinch of sugar
3 C unbleached all-purpose flour
1 t salt
½ C warm water
  cornmeal

1. Dissolve the yeast in the water. Add the sugar. Let the yeast foam and bubble (about 10 minutes).
2. Stir in 1 cup flour. Cover with a cloth, set in a warm place, and let rise until doubled in bulk (about 1½ hours).
3. In a separate bowl, combine 2 cups flour and salt. Add the rest of the water, and beat to mix.
4. On a flat surface, squeeze the yeast sponge and the flour mixture together, adding minimal amounts of flour to prevent sticking. Knead for 10 minutes (the stiff dough will gradually turn smooth and elastic).
5. Punch down dough, and shape into a smooth, round loaf. Place on an oiled baking sheet sprinkled with cornmeal. Cover with a cloth, set in a warm place, and let rise until doubled in bulk (about 1 hour).
6. Dust with flour. Bake at 400°F for 40 minutes or until done.

Yields 1 loaf

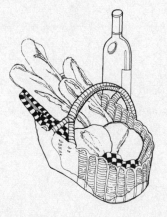

Radicchio Salad

radicchio
Boston lettuce

DRESSING
4 T safflower oil
1¾ t umeboshi
1 t white rice vinegar
½ t sesame seed oil
¼ t shredded fresh ginger (or to taste)
pinch of black pepper

1. By hand, shred enough radicchio to make four servings. Shred two to three times as much Boston lettuce. Place in a wooden salad bowl.
2. For the dressing, blend the safflower oil, umeboshi, vinegar, sesame seed oil, ginger, and pepper.
3. Immediately before serving, pour the dressing over the lettuces, and toss.

Serves 4

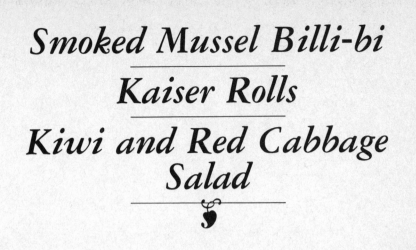

Smoked Mussel Billi-bi

Kaiser Rolls

Kiwi and Red Cabbage Salad

The Soup. This recipe provides a wonderful, fast meal for vacation time at the shore. Billi-bi (Billy-by) was created by a chef at Ciro's in Paris in 1925 and was named after a customer who preferred the mussel broth to the mussels. Now the mussels are usually either blended back into the soup or added just before serving. Smoked mussels aren't a traditional ingredient. Nevertheless, they add a fireside taste and aroma.

The Bread. You can pull homemade Kaiser Rolls apart section by section; but you can't if they're only cut on top to simulate the design, as they are in factories. These are chewy rolls that are just as good without poppy seeds or, if you prefer, use sesame seeds. You can practice with the shaping method on one roll without damaging the dough.

The Salad. Whatever these light brown, fuzzy, egg-size fruits were once called (carambola, Chinese or coromandel gooseberry), they are now named after the national bird of New Zealand, where they originally were grown. Their pale, translucent green insides (flecked with black seed patterns) set against the royal red of the cabbage makes a startling combination; and the mellow sweetness of the kiwi against the sweet-and-sour crunch of cabbage makes this salad as tasty as it looks.

Drink suggestion: ale

Smoked Mussel Billi-bi

3 T sweet butter
1 C well-washed and thinly sliced leeks (white part only)
2 t destemmed and minced parsley
¼ t thyme
1½ dozen well-scrubbed fresh mussels
2 C vinho verde (young Portuguese white wine)
1 C water
cheesecloth
smoked tinned mussels (3.66 oz), well drained
1 C heavy cream

1. Melt the butter in a saucepan over medium-low heat.
2. Add the leeks, parsley, and thyme.
3. Cover them, and simmer for 5 minutes.
4. Make sure the mussels are same-day fresh and well scrubbed with a stiff brush. Discard any open mussels. Squeeze the shell. If it opens even a crack, throw it away. Trim off the beard (threadlike material) with scissors.
5. Place the mussels in a large soup kettle with the wine and water, adding the cooked leeks and herbs.
6. Bring them to a boil over high heat. Turn the heat to medium, cover the kettle, and boil them for 8 minutes.
7. Now, the inverse rule applies. Any mussels that *did not* open should be discarded. This is a sure sign they shouldn't be eaten.

8. Drain the wine broth through several layers of cheesecloth into a bowl.
9. Pick the mussel meat from the shells, and add it to the broth. Discard the shells.
10. Spread the smoked mussels on paper towels to drain off all the oil.
11. Add the smoked mussels and heavy cream to the broth.
12. Return the Billi-bi to a large saucepan, and heat it just to the boiling point. Ladle both fresh and smoked mussels into each dish. Pour the broth over the mussels.

Serves 4

Kaiser Rolls

1 T yeast
1 C warm water
  pinch of sugar
1½ t salt
3 C unbleached all-purpose flour
  cornmeal
1 egg white
1 T warm water
2 T poppy seeds

1. Dissolve the yeast in the water.
2. Add the sugar and salt.
3. Stir in the flour, place on a flat surface, and knead 8 to 10 minutes.
4. Place dough in an oiled bowl, turn over so the top is coated with oil, cover with a cloth, and let rise in a warm spot until doubled in bulk (about 1½ hours).

5. Punch down dough, and form into a cylinder. Cut off eight equal parts.
6. To form the rolls, flatten each part with your hand on a flat surface to about a 6-inch circle; the dough will be thin. Fold one side to overlap the center point slightly. With your fingertip, press the folded edge firmly to seal. Lift the right point of this folded edge straight up and over to the center point of the dough; this slightly overlaps the previously folded part. Firmly press this point with your fingertip into the dough, and press the newly folded edge. Repeat with each of the edge points five times so that the finished roll has five folded, curved sections to it.
7. Place the rolls 2 inches apart on an oiled baking sheet sprinkled with cornmeal. Cover with a cloth, and let rise in a warm place until doubled in bulk (about 30 minutes).
8. Brush with room-temperature egg white beaten with 1 tablespoon of warm water. Sprinkle generously with poppy seeds.
9. On the bottom oven shelf, place a large, flat pan of boiling water. Bake the rolls on the center shelf at 400°F for 15 minutes or until done. Cool on a wire rack.

Yields 8 rolls

Kiwi and Red Cabbage Salad

2 C finely shredded red cabbage
2 kiwis, peeled and thinly sliced (12 slices to a fruit)

DRESSING
4 T olive oil
1 T fresh lime juice
1 t sugar
pinch of salt

1. Place the cabbage in a bowl, and cover with water for 30 minutes.
2. Drain and dry completely.
3. Arrange the cabbage on four salad plates. Decoratively overlap kiwi slices on the cabbage.
4. Mix the oil, lime juice, sugar, and salt. Pour judiciously over the salad.

Serves 4

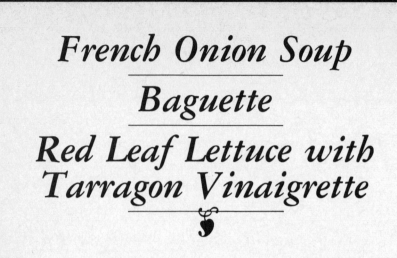

French Onion Soup

Baguette

Red Leaf Lettuce with Tarragon Vinaigrette

The Soup. When Les Halles still operated in Paris, the "in" thing to do was to stay up all night just to savor a bowl of the French onion soup. This cook's insomnious night at Les Halles left the memory of a watery, tepid soup with very soggy croutons. In our version, the toasted day-old bread rounds stay crisp, and the cream adds a smooth flavor to the onion broth. From the casserole or skillet, ladle the soup into individual au gratin bowls or ramekins.

The Bread. Crusty on the outside, soft on the inside, this is a French-type loaf for the onion soup as well as a general table bread. Cut the diagonal slits on the top deeply enough so that as the loaves bake the deepest part of the slit remains less browned than the rest of the loaf, making the baguette all the more appealing. If you use an egg yolk with water instead of the egg white for the glaze, the crust darkens to a mahogany color.

The Salad. Look for tender young lettuce with perfect leaves and a fine virgin olive oil to go with it. Look, too, for the vinegars with 7 percent acid and a tarragon stem and leaves inside the bottle, lending the natural flavor rather than only diluted tarragon extract to the vinegar.

Drink suggestion: St. Emilion wine

French Onion Soup

2 extra large onions
4 T sweet butter
5 t beef extract
5 C water
¼ C dry red wine
½ C cream
1 crusty baguette, sliced into 1-inch-thick pieces
and left standing a day
½ C grated Parmesan or Romano cheese

1. Slice the peeled onions into ¼-inch slices, cutting parallel to the top.
2. Melt the butter in an 8- or 10-inch iron skillet or ovenproof casserole.
3. Add the onions. Cover them, and simmer 5 to 8 minutes or until they are limp.
4. Stir in the beef extract, and add water.
5. Bring the broth to a boil. Reduce the heat; cover, and slowly boil the soup for 25 minutes.
6. Add the wine. While the soup simmers another 5 minutes, toast the bread on both sides under the broiler.
7. Take the skillet off the burner, and let the soup sit for 2 to 3 minutes. Stir in the cream.
8. Float toasted French bread on top of the soup, and sprinkle generously with Parmesan cheese. Reserve a little of the cheese to serve in a small dish at the table.
9. Place the soup under the broiler until the top layer of cheese sizzles (approximately 2 minutes).

Serves 4

Baguette

1 T yeast
½ C warm water
1 t salt
½ C water
2 C unbleached all-purpose flour
cornmeal

GLAZE
1 egg white
1 T water

1. Dissolve the yeast in the warm water in a bread bowl.
2. Add the salt and the rest of the water.
3. Stir in 1 cup of flour. Mix in the rest of the flour.
4. Place dough on a flat surface and knead for 8 to 10 minutes until smooth and elastic, adding flour to prevent sticking.
5. Place the dough in an oiled bowl, turn over so the top is coated with oil, cover with a cloth, and let rise in a warm spot until doubled in bulk (about 1½ hours).
6. Punch down dough, remove from the bowl, and divide it into two equal parts.
7. With a rolling pin, flatten each part into a rectangle less than ½ inch thick. With your hands, roll the dough from the long side into a tight loaf. Pinch the ends together and tuck them under the loaf, rounding off the end points. Pinch the seam the entire length of the loaf, forming the seam into a straight line.
8. Place the loaf seam-side down on a large, oiled baking sheet sprinkled with cornmeal. Cover and let rise until doubled in bulk (about 30 to 60 minutes).
9. With a razor blade or sharp knife, slit the top of each loaf in thirds with diagonal, ¾-inch-deep slashes.
10. For the glaze, brush the loaves with a mixture of egg white and water beaten together. Place a large, shallow pan of boiling water on the lower shelf of the oven.

11. Bake the loaves at 400°F for 25 to 30 minutes or until done. Five minutes before the loaves are done, brush the tops again with the egg glaze. Cool the loaves on a wire rack or serve warm.

Yields 2 loaves

Red Leaf Lettuce with Tarragon Vinaigrette

red leaf lettuce for four

DRESSING
3 T olive oil
1 T tarragon vinegar
salt to taste

1. Prepare the lettuce, tearing it into a large serving bowl.
2. For the dressing, mix the oil and vinegar together. Whisk in the salt to taste. Pour over the lettuce, and mix to coat the greens. Serve at once.

Serves 4

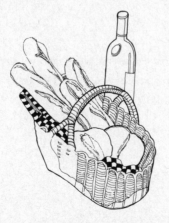

Black-eyed Pea Soup
Barley Bread
Congealed Shrimp Salad

The Soup. Southerners serve black-eyed peas (also known as cow peas) on New Year's Day. Alabamans traditionally throw a sterilized shiny silver dollar into the soup tureen for good luck. Black-eyed peas, contrary to their name, are a bean. They contribute complete protein to a meal only if you pair them with a starch, such as rice. With the addition of the brown rice, this soup constitutes a hearty, nutritional meal.

The Bread. Barley is one of the most ancient and cultivated of cereals (barley, of course, is a chief ingredient of beer). Toasting it in this recipe brings out a malty flavor in the finished loaf. Although barley dates from the Stone Age, this bread is far from a stone rendition—it's a dark-tasting, light-textured bread that is best served warm. Because barley requires and retains much water in its growth, the flour is known for its long-keeping quality. So enjoy half of the fresh loaf and know that the second half will be nearly as fresh tasting later.

The Salad. "Congealed" is the Southern description of a jelled salad, which can include virtually any array of diced vegetables, meats, fowl, and fish. The tiniest shrimp work the best in this one. If they're unavailable, simply cut the larger ones into manageable size.

Drink suggestion: lime rum shrub

Black-eyed Pea Soup

  2   C dried black-eyed peas
  4   C cold water
  1   lb smoked ham hock, leftover ham bone, or smoked ham roll
  ½   C threaded and diced celery
  ¾   C peeled and diced onion
  2   T destemmed and minced parsley
  1   clove garlic, peeled, crushed, and minced
  ¼   t cayenne
1½   t salt
  6   C water
  1   C cooked brown rice
      Southern tomato relish

1. Place the dried peas in a large soup kettle. Add 4 cups of cold water. Bring them to a boil over high heat, and boil them 2 to 3 minutes. Cover the kettle, and turn off the heat. Leave them for a few hours (or overnight) without removing the lid. This precooks the peas.
2. Add the ham hock, celery, onion, parsley, garlic, cayenne, salt, and 6 cups of water to the peas.
3. Bring them to a boil. Cover the kettle, and reduce the heat. Let the soup simmer for 1½ hours. Check periodically, and stir.
4. Remove the ham hock. Cut the ham meat off the hock or the bone and into bite-size pieces, and return it to the kettle. Taste the soup for seasoning. If the ham is salty, the soup shouldn't need any more salt.
5. Add more water if too much has boiled away. Add the cooked brown rice, and heat the soup thoroughly.
6. Place a bowl of tomato relish on the table as a garnish.

Serves 4

Barley Bread

1   T yeast
1½ C warm water
1   C toasted barley flour
1½ t salt
2   T oil
1   T unsulphured molasses
1   C whole wheat
1½ C unbleached all-purpose flour
       sweet butter

1. Dissolve the yeast in the water in a large mixing bowl.
2. In an iron skillet over medium heat, using a whisk and watching closely, stir the barley flour until the barley turns to a tan color. Remove from the heat, and cool.
3. Stir the salt, oil, and molasses into the yeast mixture.
4. Blend in the barley, whole wheat, and all-purpose flours.
5. Place on a flat surface and knead 10 minutes, adding all-purpose flour to prevent sticking.
6. Form into an oblong shape, and place seam downward in an oiled 8½ x 4½ x 2½-inch glass baking dish. Cover with a cloth, and let rise in a warm place until doubled in bulk (about 1½ hours).
7. Bake at 375°F for about 50 to 60 minutes or until done. Cool on a wire rack; brush with softened sweet butter.

Yields 1 loaf

Congealed Shrimp Salad

1 T unflavored gelatin
1 T lime juice
1 C hot water
½ t salt
1 t grated fresh onion juice
1 t hot chile sauce
2 T mayonnaise
⅓ C diced celery
¼ C diced sweet red pepper
½ t capers
1 hard-boiled egg, chopped
1 lb boiled, shelled, and deveined tiny shrimp
lettuce greens

1. Soften the gelatin in the lime juice. Add the hot water, and stir to dissolve the gelatin.
2. Add the salt, onion juice, and chile sauce. Chill to the consistency of unbeaten egg whites (about 45 to 60 minutes).
3. Fold in the mayonnaise, celery, red pepper, capers, egg, and shrimp.
4. Pour into a lightly greased 3-cup mold, and chill until firm.
5. Unmold onto a serving platter, and garnish with greens.

Serves 4

Kishik
Pistachio Lamb Bread
Eggplant Salad

The Soup. Kishik, kishk, or kishek, depending on the translation, is a Near Eastern food produced by mixing ground bulghur wheat with yogurt, letting it dry in the sun, and sieving it into a fine powder. Look for this distinct, unusual substance in stores specializing in Near Eastern foods. It tends to be expensive. Kishik has a strong odor and taste that probably won't appeal to everyone. Still, it's worth a try in order to sample a cultural food staple prevalent in Syria and other Near Eastern countries.

The Bread. Cut the bread into 1-inch-wide strips and then cut in half again for easy eating. The anise gives this a vibrant aroma and taste, while the pistachios, the greenish, delicate nuts associated so closely with Middle Eastern cooking, round out the flavors. One reason that Middle Eastern food evokes such taste memories is the happy use of herbs and spices. Don't be shy with the anise and basil.

The Salad. Vegetable, fruit, and nuts are all featured in this salmagundi salad. Although eggplant was once considered poisonous, it's now a satiny-tasting vegetable versatile enough to bread and sauté, roll and stuff, slice and layer, and, of course, steam and cube.

Drink suggestion: fresh lemonade

Kishik

¼ C virgin olive oil
1 C peeled and minced onion
1 clove garlic, peeled, crushed, and minced
⅔ C kishik
6 C chicken broth
black pepper, freshly ground
2 hard-boiled eggs
⅓ C destemmed and minced parsley

1. In a large, heavy skillet, heat the olive oil over medium heat; and add the onion and garlic. Sauté them for a few minutes. Reduce the heat to low, cover the onions, and let them sweat 5 to 8 minutes or until limp.
2. Stir in the kishik, and slowly add 5 cups of the chicken broth. Stir, and bring the kishik to a boil. Reduce to a simmer, and cook 7 minutes while stirring. The soup will become fairly thick. Add the remaining cup of chicken broth and the pepper.
3. Peel and chop the eggs. Mix the eggs with parsley, and serve them as a garnish on each portion.

Serves 6

Pistachio Lamb Bread

2 T yeast
½ C warm water
1½ C water
1 T salt
  pinch of sugar
2 T oil
5 to 6 C unbleached all-purpose flour
  cornmeal

TOPPING
1 T oil
1 small garlic clove
½ C chopped onion
½ lb ground lamb
  salt and pepper to taste
  pinch of basil
  generous pinch of aniseed
¼ C chopped pistachio nuts
¼ C chopped parsley
  olive oil

1. For the bread, dissolve the yeast in the warm water. Add the 1½ cups water, salt, sugar, and oil.
2. Beat in 3 cups of flour. Stir in the rest of the flour. Place on a flat surface; knead for 8 to 10 minutes, adding flour to prevent sticking.
3. Place dough in an oiled bowl, turn over so the top is coated with oil, cover with a cloth, and let rise in a warm spot until doubled in bulk (about 1½ hours). Meanwhile, prepare the topping (step 6).
4. Punch down dough, place on a flat surface, and shape into a cylinder. Cut into equal halves. At this point, decide to make six or twelve servings. If six, reserve one-half of the dough for a different loaf, and cut the other half into six equal parts.

5. With your hands, round each part into a ball; then flatten it between your palms. Then on a floured flat surface and with a rolling pin, roll the dough into 5-inch rounds.

6. For the topping, heat the oil in an iron skillet, add the garlic and onions, and cover until cooked. Remove the mixture with a slotted spoon, leaving the oil behind; and set aside.

7. Fry the lamb in the same skillet, chopping the meat into fine pieces with a wooden spoon. Mix in the salt, pepper, basil, and anise seed. Cook the lamb until done. Pour off excess fat.

8. Combine the lamb mixture with the onion mixture. Add the pistachios and parsley.

9. To assemble, place the flattened rounds of dough on an oiled baking sheet sprinkled with cornmeal. Spoon the lamb mixture onto the bread rounds. Sprinkle generously with olive oil.

10. Bake at 425°F for 15 to 20 minutes or until done, when the edges of the bread rounds are lightly toasted.

Yields 6 (or 12) rounds

Eggplant Salad

5 C peeled and cubed eggplant
2 scallions (bottom 3 inches), chopped
½ C diced celery
½ C peeled, cored, and diced apple
½ C chopped pecans
½ C destemmed chopped parsley

DRESSING
¼ C olive oil
1½ T cider vinegar
¼ t dried thyme
3 T unflavored yogurt
salt and pepper to taste

green leaf lettuce

1. Steam the eggplant until tender (about 10 to 15 minutes). Place it in a strainer, drain, and cool.
2. Prepare the scallions, celery, apple, pecans, and parsley. Place them in a bowl, add the eggplant, and mix.
3. For the dressing, mix the oil, vinegar, thyme, yogurt, salt, and pepper. Pour over the salad, and stir. Chill. Place on a bed of lettuce, and serve.

Serves 4

Fromage de Chèvre Soup
Honey Wheat Rolls
Tomatoes Vinaigrette

The Soup. Carefully select the goat cheese for this soup. A cheese such as feta, sold at most delicatessen counters, doesn't melt well, probably due to added ingredients and/or preservatives. The goat cheese must be creamy (not crumbly), such as the Italian Latte di Capra, Caprini di Capra, or the French Bûchette. Fromage de Chèvre Soup has a distinctive, stimulating flavor that whets the appetite for more. Serve it hot or cold.

The Bread. For their wholesome, nutty flavor, old-fashioned whole wheat rolls are perfect. These have a lightness to them that combines with the hearty wheat flavor. Medium-coarse stone-ground flour makes the difference. You can also bake this recipe as a loaf, preferably as a round on a baking sheet to get as much crust as possible.

The Salad. Garden-plucked, juicy, sweetened-on-the-vine, blazing red tomatoes are essential for this mouth-watering salad to be its best. Placed on a white platter with bright green parsley scattered generously on top, such a simple plate of tomatoes becomes a centerpiece for the appetite. Although you can serve it at once, try to prepare it two or three hours ahead of time to allow the tomatoes to marinate in the vinaigrette. You may be tempted to refrigerate the salad, but we find that keeping it at room temperature heightens its taste as well as deterring the oil from solidifying.

Drink suggestion: Cabernet rosé wine

Fromage de Chevre Soup

¾ lb destemmed string beans (snap into pieces)
2 C chicken broth
2 T sweet butter
¼ C finely diced onion
½ lb cream-style goat cheese

1. Steam the string beans in a vegetable steamer over boiling water, covered, for 20 minutes.
2. Place the chicken broth and string beans in a blender or food processor, and purée them for 1 minute. Pour the purée into a medium-size saucepan.
3. Melt the butter in another small saucepan. Add the onions, and sauté them over medium heat for 2 to 3 minutes. Cover the onions, lower the heat, and let them sweat until golden (5 to 8 minutes).
4. Purée the onions in the blender or food processor with some of the string bean purée. Add the onion mixture to the rest of the bean purée.
5. Heat the soup to just below boiling, but do not boil it.
6. Cut the creamy goat cheese into small slices. Add them to the string bean mixture, and whisk the soup as the cheese melts.
7. When the cheese is completely melted, the soup is ready to serve.

Serves 4

Honey Wheat Rolls

1 T yeast
1 C warm water
1½ t salt
1 T oil
1 T honey
1 extra large egg, beaten
1 C stone-ground whole wheat
2 C unbleached all-purpose flour
toasted wheat germ
sweet butter, melted

1. Dissolve the yeast in the water.
2. Stir in the salt, oil, honey, and egg.
3. Beat in the flours. Knead on a flat surface 8 to 10 minutes until smooth and elastic, adding all-purpose flour to prevent sticking.
4. Form the dough into a round, place in an oiled bowl, turn the dough over so the top is coated with the oil, cover with a cloth, and let rise in a warm spot until doubled in bulk (about 1½ hours).
5. Punch down dough, and form into a cylinder. Divide into sixteen equal parts. Form the rolls by tucking the dough into the center of itself continuously until you've made a smooth ball. Place the rolls seam-side down and evenly spaced (with one roll in the center) in two oiled, round 8-inch cake pans. Cover with a cloth, and let rise until doubled in bulk (30 to 45 minutes).
6. Bake at 375°F for 20 minutes or until done. Ten minutes before done, remove from the oven and brush with water. Sprinkle toasted wheat germ on top, and return to finish baking. Brush with melted sweet butter.

Yields 16 rolls

Tomatoes Vinaigrette

3 to 4 vine-ripened tomatoes

DRESSING
3 T olive oil
1½ t balsamic vinegar
¼ t imported oregano leaves
⅛ t salt or to taste
pinch of pepper
2 T destemmed chopped parsley

1. Carefully slice tomatoes into rounds ¼ inch thick. Overlap them slightly to cover most of a platter.
2. For the dressing, combine the oil, vinegar, oregano, salt, and pepper. Whisk to blend, and pour over the tomatoes.
3. Sprinkle with parsley, and serve.

Serves 4 to 6

Green Chile Soup
Chile and Cheese Cornbread
Jicama Salad

The Soup. Although the chiles are mild, the lips of the diner might sizzle a little, so servings should be fairly small. The jicama salad cuts the bite of the chiles.

The Bread. The fresh yellow corn, red pimiento, and green chile make an appealing confetti wedge of cornbread on your plate. This version has a very mild taste of chile; and by not overcooking the bread, you'll find it moist and light. Take the black cast iron skillet (with *no* wooden handle) straight from the oven to the table to serve the wedges. The skillet keeps the bread warm for additional servings as well as provides a centerpiece.

The Salad. Popular in Mexico and increasingly here, jicama (pronounced *hee*-ka-ma) is a refreshing cross between the texture of a radish without the peppery taste and the moist crispness of a mild, cold apple. This is a do-it-yourselfer salad according to individual taste—squeeze the lime juice over the slices, and add more chile sauce, if desired. It's an easily prepared salad.

Drink suggestion: Mexican beer

Green Chile Soup

   2 *T sweet butter*
   ½ *C peeled and minced onion*
   ¼ *t cumin*
   6 *oz cream cheese*
   1 *C drained and chopped prepared mild green chiles*
 1¼ *C chicken broth*

1. Melt the butter in a medium-size saucepan over low heat.
2. Add the onions and cumin.
3. Cover and sweat the onions 5 to 8 minutes until they're golden.
4. In a food processor, blend the cream cheese and chiles until they are smooth.
5. Add the onions, and process the mixture well for 2 to 3 minutes.
6. Place the chile mixture in a saucepan with the chicken broth, and heat but don't boil the soup.

Serves 4

Chile and Cheese Cornbread

2 ears fresh corn (about 1½ C kernels)
3 T sweet butter
3 T heavy cream
1 C yellow cornmeal
½ C unbleached all-purpose flour
1 T baking powder
1 t salt
2 eggs, very well beaten
1 C sour cream
½ C chopped mild prepared green chiles
2 T chopped pimiento
¼ C corn oil
1½ C shredded cheddar cheese

1. Shuck the corn, and remove the silky threads. Using a sharp knife, cut off the kernels into a pan or other container.
2. Melt the butter in a skillet, and sauté the corn for 5 minutes, stirring frequently. Remove from heat, and stir in the cream. Set aside.
3. In a large mixing bowl, combine the cornmeal, flour, baking powder, and salt.
4. Add the eggs, sour cream, chiles, pimiento, and oil. Blend well. Stir in the corn mixture.
5. Spread half of the mixture on a greased 8-inch iron skillet. Sprinkle on the cheese. Spread on the rest of the mixture.
6. Bake at 375°F for 25 to 30 minutes or until done. Serve warm in the skillet, remembering to lift the skillet with a thick pot holder.

Serves 6 to 8

Jicama Salad

1 jicama
1 lime, quartered
   hot chile sauce to taste

1. Peel the jicama, and cut it in half. Slice thinly into manageable size (about ¼ inch or less), and artfully place the slices on clear-glass or dark-colored plates.
2. Place a lime quarter in the center of the jicama. Chill.
3. Before serving, dot several slices with hot red chile sauce.

Serves 4

Glossary

Al dente. Firm to the bite; usually used when speaking about pasta.

Arrowroot. Thickening agent extracted from tropical tubers and root-stocks.

Balsamic vinegar. An aged Italian vinegar.

Béchamel. A white sauce made with flour, butter, and milk.

Belgian endive. A 4-inch-long cylinder of compact, tart, white leaves tinged with pale green on the tips; used for salads and often braised as a hot vegetable.

Bibb lettuce. The finest of the butterhead lettuces.

Bock beer. Made with malt and hops; produced to appear the first day of spring.

Bok choy. Chinese cabbage with dark green leaves.

Boston lettuce. One of the finer butterhead lettuces, with smooth leaves.

Bouquet garni. Herbs, such as thyme, bay leaf, and parsley, tied in a small cheesecloth bag so they can be removed easily after cooking.

Brut champagne. Drier than extra dry champagne.

Capers. Buds from the caper bush of the Mediterranean; usually pickled in brine.

Caviar. Roe, or eggs, from the female fish; beluga comes from the sturgeon, although other popular caviar comes from lumpfish, salmon, and cod.

Cayenne. A red powder made from hot chile and named for French Guiana's Cayenne.

Chiffonade. Shredded vegetables.

Cilantro. Coriander, a sparse-leaf plant known as Chinese parsley.

Cioppino. A spicy fish stew.

Clarify. To make broth clear by adding egg whites, which attract the cloudy particles; clarified butter is slowly melted so that the solids drop to the bottom and the clear fat can be poured off.

Congealed. A Southern term for jelled or gelatin salad.

Consommé. A clear stock made from beef or fowl.

Couscousier. A special double boiler used to steam couscous.

Extra dry champagne. Sweeter than brut champagne.

Finocchio. Italian for fennel; also known as Florentine fennel.

Food mill. This utensil grinds and purées foods.

Food processor. A multipurpose appliance that chops, mixes, blends, pulverizes, and purées at high speed and power when specifically designed blades are inserted.

Fumet. A fish broth made with bones and the trimmings.

Gumbo. A thick, Cajun, okra-based soup or stew.

Jicama. A dark, rough-skinned Mexican tuber that, when peeled and sliced, tastes like a turnip or apple.

Julienne. Vegetables cut into matchstick-thin pieces.

Kielbasa. A type of Polish sausage flavored with garlic.

Lager. A light beer.

Linguiça. Portuguese spiced sausage.

Lox. Smoked salmon found at most fish markets and delicatessens.

Mezza luna. A half moon–shaped cutting tool that is rocked back and forth to chop ingredients.

Miso. A cooked and fermented soybean paste used in Oriental dishes.

Plump. To round out dried fruit by rehydrating them, as done by soaking raisins in a liquid.

Purée. To blend into a smooth consistency.

Radicchio. A smallish head of tart, red-purplish and white leaves used in salads.

Ramekin. An individual baking dish.

Render. To extract the oil or fat by cooking.

Roux. A liaison of flour and fat or butter used as a thickening agent.

Salsa. Mexican sauce.

Scungilli. Italian name for sea whelk; conch.

Seviche. Raw fish marinated in lime juice, which "cooks" the fish by the natural acid.

Sin choy. Chinese celery cabbage with light green leaves.

Split. A bottle of wine approximately half the size of the standard bottle.

Sweat. To cover vegetables and allow them to steam in their own juices.

Sweet butter. Unsalted butter.

Tabasco. A sauce made from the capisum chile pepper. The sauce is a brand made and bottled on Avery Island, Louisiana.

Thread. To remove the undigestible "strings" of celery.

Umeboshi. Salted Japanese red plum vinegar.

Unbleached all-purpose flour. White flour that has not been bleached with several possible peroxides to whiten the flour even more.

Vichyssoise. A chilled cream soup made with leeks and potatoes.

Vinaigrette. A salad dressing made, generally, of 3 to 4 parts oil to 1 part vinegar, with salt and pepper, and sometimes mustard.

Wild rice. A tall native grass producing seeds that resemble rice; it grows primarily in Michigan, Minnesota, and Wisconsin and is gathered mostly by native Americans.

Winter melon. A variety of melon used by the Chinese.

Alphabetical Listing
of Recipes

The Soups

The Breads

The Salads

Index

Cranberry juice, 76
Cranberry Orange Loaf, 37, 39–40
Cranberry Salad, Chicken, 195, 198
Craneberry, 195
Cream of Artichoke and Prosciutto Soup, 84–85
Cream of Vegetable Soup, 93–94, 99
Cream Rolls, 130–32
Creamy Butterbean Soup, 2, 138–39
Crocus, 32
Croissants, 7, 155, 157–58
Crumpets, 89, 91–92
Cucumber Salad, 9, 57, 60
Cucumber Soup (Cold), Persian, 199–200
Curries, 125
Cusk, 19

Daikon Salad, 101, 103–104
Dandelion greens, 190
Deviled Eggs, 169, 172
Dressings (salads)
    bacon, 52, 145
    cheese, 113
    green goddess, 118
    lime, 137, 214
    mayonnaise, 15
    Mexican salsa, 189
    onion, 48
    remoulade, 92
    rice vinegar, 185
    sour cream, 60
    sweet and sour, 140–41
    tahini, 153
    tarragon vinaigrette, 129
    tomato, 69
    umebashi (Japanese), 210
    vinaigrette, 15
    yogurt, 129, 149, 227
Duck
    broth, 4
    wild, 32
Duck Gumbo, 32–34

Earl Grey tea, 89
Egg Bread and Rye Loaf, 66, 68–69
Egg cream, 138
Eggplant, 81
Eggplant Salad, 224, 227–28

Eggs, Deviled, 169, 172
Emerson, 6
Endive and Escarole Salad, 190, 193–94
Endive Salad, Belgian, 8
English muffins, 89
Escarole Salad, Endive and, 190, 193–94

Felafel, 173
Fennel, 19
Fennel Salad, 8, 22
Feta (goat cheese), 80, 82, 229
Feta Crescents, 80, 82
Finocchio, 19
Fish, 19
    broth, 4
    salmon, 66
    stew (Cioppino), 19
    Wing of Lox Soup, 66
Fish stock, 12–13
Fishmonger, 4, 66
Flat breads, Armenian, 27
"Flipper dough" (Portuguese fried dough), 146
Florentine fennel, 19
French bread, 216
    baguette, 218–19
French Market, 32
French Onion Soup, 216–17
French toast, 207
French Wreath Bread, 61, 63–64
Fried Bread, 45–47
Fried Plantain Soup, 169–70
Fried Scallion Cakes, 181, 183–84
Fromage de Chevre Soup, 2, 229–30
Fruit Salad, 71, 74–75
Fruit Salad, Tropical, 8, 125, 128–29
Fruit soup, 160
Fumet, 12–13

Garnishes, 4–5
Gazpacho, Baja, 45–46
Gelatin, 84
Goat cheese soup, 2, 229–30
Gold Book, The, 3
Golden Saffron Buns, 169, 171
Gombo, 32
Gorgonzola and Apple Salad, 8, 110, 113